THE BORIMOL PLAINS

Written by
Lady Elderies Saldalgiar

Translated into the Berillai by
Lord Terin Durisal

The Historical Context of the Borimol Plains:
A Brief Primer

To my dearest readers, you have my sincerest thanks for your selection

of this humble volume! As I have often said, it is a shame our people

know so little of the storied literature of the Continent. However, I

hope that you find this translation of Lady Saldalgiar's seminal work

not only informative but *inspiring*, too. There is an immense richness

to Anushai society that I hope to share with you, a wellspring of

culture that only adds to the beautiful intricacy of our own.

However, I know that for many of my readers, Anushai also

remains an opaque and fearsome nation, not least of all for the

centrality of Shapewalkers in their government. Thus, to provide both

cultural and historical context, I hoped to write this briefest of primers

to explain not only Anushai, but the context in which this novel was

written.

The Erril Basin
Under the Golden Empire

On the next page is a map of the Golden Empire at its height. I think it

no coincidence that this period also coincided with the zenith of

Anushai literature. This book was written in the year 950 in the

Anushai calendar (61 PN in the Berillai). And as you can see, this was before King Rummon sailed across the seas to found our great

kingdom. In this period, the borders were far looser with almost every

nation serving as a mere gem in the Anushai crown. There is some

mention in this book of a conflict in Alara, which I believe refers to the

Highland Wars, a bloody contest, which took place around the year

915.

The Anushai House System

Equally vital to understanding the context of this novel is the system of government in Anushai. According to their tradition, their ruling class is divided into 10 houses. This stems from their religious tradition. Unlike our own worship of the true gods, many in Anushai believe in a folkloric deity known as "Essomuai." They believe that the ten houses descend from the goddess's children, and the heads of these houses partake in a voting ritual to decide their emperor or empress depending on the needs of the kingdom. Beyond this, each house had a vital role to play in the organs of the empire's government and administration, a practice that in many way remains to this day. As you will see in the novel, our heroine, Vorseyai Shuwayel, is of the Grass House lineage. Their sigil, which I recreated in an etching during one of my many journeys to Anushai, is included on the next page. If you find such anthropological tidbits of interest, I suggest you read *Empire & Artifact* by Sir Arteir Pallinayum.

I do so hope you enjoy taking this journey with me. I have always found this novel to be a delight, not least of all because it was the first novel I read in the high form of Anushai. It is considered a classic by our neighbors to the north, and I hope it will become equally as dear to you.

-Lord Terin Durisal

1

Vorseyai looked out at the sweeping fields of Borimol, watching as the wind pulled at the long grass baking in the afternoon sun. Huge thunderclouds gathered in the distance, their dark shadows rising like castles in the air. She idly fingered Mother's moonstone necklace, sighing as she thought of the woman for the hundredth time. Even after all this mourning, it was hard to believe she'd really died, that anyone on Mother's side of the family was capable of an act so frivolous as *dying*. The necklace was delicate, everything Mother wasn't — at least, before the end — its spun gold woven carefully together and studded with nearly two dozen stones. Still, its weight was soothing, a reminder of what still remained.

She shielded her eyes and looked out at the horizon, finding the sun already tilting toward the west. Another day wasted … The summers in Yuljeom were already too brief as it was, the county's place on the coast somehow dumping it with even more rain than the capital. It was only in the brief window of summer when a year's worth of balls, hunts, and Shaping competitions would be held, all of it jammed in before everyone went to town. Thank Essomuai her mourning was finally over! If she had to miss Baron Jullil's ball tomorrow on top of all the others, she may well have shown up in black, propriety be damned.

Not that she was so crass as to not mourn Mother — far from it. She would miss the woman every second of every day for the rest of her life. If anything, it was Mother herself who made her itch to be free of the black clothes. Very much in accordance with her nature, in her last moments, Mother had clutched her hand, boring into her with glassy, half-closed eyes.

"Not a day more of mourning than you must," she'd said. "Promise me."

Vorseyai had promised, of course. And even if she didn't exactly feel like dancing, she *did* feel like making progress on her more sacred vow:

to marry well in Mother's absence. Unfortunately, to accomplish such a task, one simply had to attend the balls, and over twenty as she was, even dreaded hosts like Baron Jullil were too precious to pass up.

Somewhere behind her, a clock chimed the hour. It was time to do her rounds for the day — such as were allowed to a baroness in mourning, anyway. At least she could change the order, alternating between touring the gardens and visiting the temple in town. Today, she may as well start out back before the rain came — not that she knew what to do with half of Father's bloody plants … Still, Borimol was hers now, and the staff deserved to see her at the helm.

Besides, for all her complaining, it really did give her some measure of peace to walk among the plants. The grounds of Borimol had been tended by her house for generations, after all. And even if Mother and Father had waged countless battles over the greenhouse — and the fortune Father spent on it — in the end it was the closest thing she had to a monument, the only place she could find the lost without traveling to Mount Seongbelm.

She stood, gathering her skirts as she pushed herself up from Father's old rattan chair. As she crossed the veranda, the younger footman, Oeurelai, was already there, opening the door into the house. He kept his eyes straight and his posture erect, though he at least returned her nod as she passed. Most of the staff still acted as if their heads were on the block — not that she could blame them… Mother had only grown more ferocious after Father passed, and there had been no one — save Vorseyai herself — who saw them as people.

And yet, equilibrium felt a long way off. It wasn't like she could just return to the way Father had managed the house, either. The man had been well-meaning nearly to the point of driving the staff mad, not to mention his endless botany questions. As if they wanted to have their master taking notes on which herbs they used when they were sick! Still, there had to be some middle ground between harrying the staff and having them tiptoe about …

She stepped into the front hall, her lady's maid, Eserrion, already waiting for her. The stout woman had started as her governess but switched roles after her debut, claiming she wanted to see her properly wed before finding a new station. All of that suited Vorseyai perfectly well, of course — it was impossible to find a good lady's maid in Yuljeom. Though with Mother gone, she also wouldn't deny it pleased her to be mothered.

"It looks like rain, my lady," Eserrion said, falling in beside her.

"Would you like me to fetch your umbrella before your rounds?"

Vorseyai looked outside. They were on the east side of the manor now, and the large paneled windows overlooking the gardens displayed the full awe and menace of the approaching clouds. Still, she couldn't help but see them as an opportunity.

"No need," she said, grinning. "I think I'll risk it today."

Eserrion clucked her tongue.

"Well," she said, "do be careful. It doesn't become a lady to look like a drowned rat."

Vorseyai rolled her eyes, chuckling. Two mothers indeed. In fact, it was her actual mother who had trained her to forgo umbrellas in the first place. Mother always said it was worth a bit of damp to contrive a chance at gallantry. If you went without an umbrella before a rain storm, there was always the chance some refined gentleman would rescue you from the rain, whisking you into his carriage for a tête-à-tête.

"I think I'll try my luck," she said, winking at the older woman. "You know it's better to need rescuing than to miss out on love."

Eserrion sniffed at that. Sometimes it seemed it actually vexed her that she hadn't birthed Vorseyai herself. The woman *had* done the lion's share of her rearing, of course. Mother had always been more interested in house politics. Still, her love was beyond question; some things simply went with their station. A baroness did her daughter no favors with softness, after all.

"Well, don't forget propriety," Eserrion said. "There's no point in the hunt if you don't find a worthy suitor. Having the luck to save a lady from the rain does not a gentleman make."

They reached the end of the hall, finding Merishail waiting for them. The butler was standing by the sitting room, her sun hat in hand. Oeurelai must have summoned him. It seemed her daily custom really was becoming too predictable … He also held an umbrella for her, but to her credit, Eserrion narrowly shook her head. Merishail nodded subtly, placing the umbrella on the stand behind him.

"Your hat, my lady," he said, offering it to Eserrion, who carefully placed it over Vorseyai's curls before tying the bow.

"Thank you, Merishail," she said once the hat was on. "I always know I'll be cared for when you're around."

Merishail smiled widely at that. He had followed Father since their military days, all the way back to the first Alaran campaign, and loyalty like that simply couldn't be bought — whatever Mother said. Not all servants did well with encouragement, of course — they were very nearly as fussy as plants! But she knew Merishail well enough to know what would make him bloom.

If only Mother had known what she was truly in for at Borimol… The woman had settled on a match with Father without ever laying eyes on their estates. She'd probably thought no further than how Father's four thousand crowns per year would add to her own seven — with a better title, of course. She may have thought she was marrying a brilliant politician, given Grandpapa's reputation, though it couldn't have been further from the truth. Father had cared only for his servants and his plants, but Mother probably hadn't learned that until the engagement was set.

"Thank you both," she said to the servants before heading into the sitting room on her own. There was a rear veranda there leading to the gardens, and everyone seemed to understand now her need for privacy during her rounds. It had taken some coaxing to get Eserrion to go along, of course — the woman would be her shadow if she could! — but she was the head of the house now, and she needed to walk on her own.

Even in the summer, with the hearths empty, the sitting room had a cozy feeling, done up as it was in velvets and dark mahogany. This had been Father's domain, and there were still rows of his books along the walls. Mother had preferred her own study, devoid of books but perfect for her obsessive letter writing. For her, though, it was this room that felt like home. She'd spent so many nights curled up on that sofa! Even when they were joined by Father's awful botany friends, this had been the heart of the house. She walked through the room, pausing at the back door to look in the mirror on the wall.

She turned her head to and fro, considering her hat. Now that she looked at it, it didn't seem to match the dress at all. But should she change the hat or the dress? She looked down at her dress. The smooth blue silk was certainly a favorite, and it would feel better in the heat than any of her woolens. The hat then. She had one upstairs that had a delicate lace embroidery of goldenrod flowers on it that should do the trick. Still, it was hardly worth fetching a servant to retrieve it for her… She didn't know the pattern perfectly, but she'd just have to shape it for herself.

She closed her eyes and grabbed her moonstone necklace, the spun gold specifically crafted to aid in Shapewalking. It was a rare piece, and a wonder Mother's family had let it slip away. The metal was said to be from the same vein used to build the fountain in the capital. The spun gold vibrated in her fingers, aligning her heart with Essomuai. There was a dull glow, and when she opened her eyes, the hat was transformed. It wasn't exactly like the one she wanted, but it was a far better match than the pink piece Merishail had brought her. She nodded to herself in the mirror and headed out into the garden. No matter what waited for her out there, with the right hat, it could all be overcome.

2

As could be expected from a storied Grass House family, the gardens at Borimol flowed seamlessly from the back of the house. The carpeting bled right onto the gravel path, the walls giving way to enormous flower beds and gently waving willows. The house itself seemed to be the only thing breaking up the sea of green, the walls shining red with great-great-Grandpapa's terra-cotta. But lest anyone forget the family's provenance, the manor was still capped in a thick spread of turquoise tiles.

Most afternoons she would take her time wandering through the hedgerows, but with the rain on the horizon, she kept to the central path, walking past the fountains and statuaries on her way to the sprawling greenhouse at the southern edge of the grounds. The great glass structure shimmered in the afternoon heat, forcing her to shield her eyes as she looked out at it.

The greenhouse *was* a marvel, and a testament to the empire's artisans — even if it was rather an indictment of Father's lack of thrift. He'd spent a considerable part of his fortune on it, sending for the materials from all across Wellonai — glass from Relimora, iron from the Three Sisters, and even handcrafted plant beds from guild workers in Amoriai.

Still, looking at Father's palace of plants, it was hard not to admire his vision. Apparently he'd dreamt it up as a child, claiming a traveling priest had saved Grandmama with some rare herb from the south. That single moment had transformed his life, ruling the rest of his days. In the summers, he would travel the world collecting cuttings, and in the winter, he would expand the greenhouse, sometimes even forcing his men to work in the snow to make room for his latest discoveries — which, of course, littered the house before they could be transplanted.

Ironically, all his eccentricity had made him rather beloved in the village, everyone always clamoring to hear about his travels—though he always seemed baffled when they asked questions that weren't about plants. Unfortunately, his reputation for storytelling had actually attracted Mother in the beginning. She must have thought the plants were an excuse for his adventures, when the truth was quite the opposite. And now, the greenhouse was full of obscure plants, the purpose of which not even Father likely knew in full.

At least her purpose in continuing Father's dream could stretch beyond the plants themselves. In the end, his experiment had attracted some three dozen greenhouse workers to Borimol, along with the occasional visiting scholar and, of course, his botany director, Mr. Seoyaln. As she saw it, her true duty was to the staff, keeping them well employed and cared for. Much of what they harvested was commercially useless, but she still made an effort to be seen at the greenhouses every day; anything to give them — and Father's memory — the dignity they deserved.

Of course, Seoyaln would beg to differ. He seemed molded by Essomuai to vex her personally. He was apparently of rank — in what house wasn't clear — though he acted as if he would have gladly led the Kesurin Uprising himself. What was it about botany that made such zealots of men? He could be relied upon, at least, and the staff swore he treated everyone well, but he was nearly as fervent about the plants as Father had been.

She took a deep breath, girding herself for their daily battle. He was determined to send her chasing night bunnies when he could, always prattling on about the most obscure plants while imploring her to write to so-and-so to sell them. She, of course, told him to write himself and sell them for a copper if he wished. But *apparently* propriety demanded the head of the house negotiate the contracts for the useless little leaves. Even worse, he seemed to think everyone in the bloody capital would be tripping over themselves to get them!

She came to the end of the planted gardens, where the grounds opened onto a large field leading to the greenhouse. The grass there was allowed to grow high, and it swayed in the hot summer air, pushed to the south by the coming storm. She breathed deeply, the herbal scent filling her nose. Her great-great-grandmother had supposedly started growing the grass to make perfume, but it had grown out of control, quickly taking over the whole southern end.

Halfway through the field, she heard a rustle to her left, pausing as a long train of grass cats emerged, crossing the path to reach the thicket on the other side. There were about a dozen of them, not including the babies clinging to their backs. They didn't acknowledge her in the slightest and moved at the pace of mud, the mushrooms on their back bobbing about until they were out of sight. She couldn't help but chuckle.

They may have been the sigil of Grass House, but they had to be the oddest creatures in the world!

She was about to walk on when another form came rustling through the grass. She tensed, worried she'd have to drag one of the dogs away from the cat herd, but a moment later, Muylesin, one of the greenhouse workers, emerged. He didn't see her right away when he came out, wiping his forehead as he muttered under his breath. As he scanned the opposite thicket, he finally noticed her.

"Oh, m'lady," he said, pulling his hat off and bowing. "Apologies, I didn't see you there. It's just, the cats are wandering again — it's time for new kittens, you see."

"Think nothing of it," she said, smiling. "You know my opinion of them. How's your wife doing with her own new addition?"

They had a little cottage not far south of town, and had just had their … third baby? She had sent over some food a week or two back but made a mental note to send more.

"Oh, doing wonderfully, m'lady," he said. "Thank you kindly." He nodded to her again, crossing the path. "I'll be on my way, if you'll excuse me. Mr. Seoyaln wants the cats back immediately."

"Of course," she said as he disappeared into the grass in the direction the cats had taken. She chuckled, continuing on toward the greenhouse. Those fool cats … Part of why Seoyaln had been hired at Borimol was his expertise with the creatures. Father had established the herd sometime around her fifth birthday, though they'd had some thirty litters since then. Their backs were supposedly excellent at growing some rare medicine or something, but they were supremely lazy and had a penchant for wandering. The herd made Borimol look awfully silly, but it had been in her father's will they not be removed, so on they stayed, eternally wandering and proliferating.

Finally, she approached the entrance to the greenhouse, the glass still revealing an interior jungle despite the shimmering sun. Every day she seemed to forget anew how massive it was, nearly as wide as the manor itself and half as long, divided into sections based on the type of plant in question. There were two more workers taking clippings from the exterior plants, both of them scrambling up to bow as they noticed her.

"Afternoon, m'lady," they said in unison.

"Calinaem, Zemshin," she said, nodding in return. One of them moved hastily to open the door, bowing her through.

She walked into a wall of humidity, blinking as she wrinkled her nose. Something was always bloody flowering in the place, though it seemed particularly pungent today … She was tempted to reach for her handkerchief, but it would be better not to blot her makeup before the temple. At least she'd used that quality rouge from Relimora, so she knew it wouldn't run from the heat alone.

Her eyes scanned across the wings of the greenhouse, passing over plants that could very well have been from another planet altogether. The first room was full of ferns, buckets of water in the corners letting out the humidity as they baked in the sun. She finally caught sight of Seoyaln through the glass, tending to the plants in the dry room. With any luck, she could keep him in there where she wouldn't feel like a roast pheasant.

The dry room was full of peculiar tube-shaped plants with spikes, supposedly from the eastern corner of Ekosinar near the Void. Seoyaln claimed their flowers had very potent effects, though she'd never seen them blossom herself. He was bent over one of the shorter ones, his nose very nearly caught in the spikes. He wasn't wearing a coat under his leather apron, through he still had a proper gingham vest over well-tailored trousers. She walked to the center of the room, but he still didn't look up from his business.

"Mr. Seoyaln," she said lightly.

"Ah, Vorseyai," he said, continuing as he was.

Irksome man! He was of rank, so technically he could use her name, but he was still in her employ. She honestly preferred a casual *m'lady* to such vulgar familiarity. But without knowing his exact rank, she didn't exactly have grounds to push the issue. Sometimes he seemed too gallant by half, tripping over himself to help her with a puddle, while other times he barely seemed to know her from one of his ferns. It made her wonder where he'd been educated — and which bloody house he was from, for that matter. His home was supposedly somewhere in the northwest, which could mean anything really … Knowing Father, she probably shouldn't judge the man from his habits, but really!

Finally, he finished what he was doing, making a few notes in his ledger before standing and giving her a small bow.

"Thank you for coming," he said — which he, of course, said every day. She simply nodded, and he turned, leading her deeper into the greenhouse.

"I thought I'd show you some of the woodshear crop," he said as they wound through the desert plants toward the forest room. If she wasn't forgetting, the woodshear was some mushroom he'd been cultivating all summer. He'd already shown her a few months prior, but he did seem more enthusiastic about them than even his normal adoration called for.

"I'd very much like it if you wrote to Lord Elkurae in town now that they're ready," he said. "I met him last season, and he had a most interesting study in Amoriai on diseases of the bone. I think he'd sign a contract if you put it by him. It was a year ago, of course, but I told him it was on my list of specimens for this summer, and he was very keen to hear it."

Vorseyai continued behind him but stopped listening as she stared into the plants. She did make a note to write the letter, though she gave no acknowledgment of it. She wrote to maybe one in four of the lords and ladies he suggested — mostly to keep him guessing, though she also wanted to avoid overextending the estate with his schemes. She had managed Father in much the same way, always giving him an outlet but not always following through on his harebrained plots.

Thankfully, the forest room was no hotter than the gardens, the windows open to the breeze. They followed a curving path around the bushes and saplings until they came to a hollowed-out recess in the ground. There, among the roots of a large conifer, was a large swath of the purple woodshear. They had at least tripled in size since he last showed her, so at least he was properly cultivating the blasted things … They did have an enchanting color, though their actual potency in medicine seemed questionable — Lord Elkurae notwithstanding.

Seoyaln scrambled down into the hole and took a knife from his belt, taking a cutting from one of the mushrooms and handing it up to her. She looked at it for a moment before finally pulling out her handkerchief and taking the thing.

"What am I to make of it?" she asked, staring at the purple blob in her hand.

"Smell it," he said. She arched an eyebrow at him, but he kept that same innocent look on his face. She shook her head, raising it to her nose. It smelled like … roses? Not at all what you'd expect of a fungus.

"Good, right?" he asked, a wide smile on his face. "That's how you know they're ready for healing. They smell quite like feet before they're mature — not useful in the slightest. But now … Well, that's why I'd like you to write. We have a few weeks to harvest and dry them, but I think they'll be quite successful."

She looked at the mushroom a while longer, suddenly thinking of Father. He would have smiled like that, too, had he seen the woodshear.

"Mr. Seoyaln," she said, handing the purple blob back. "I do thank you for everything you've done here. Honoring my father's work like this … well, it's more than I could ask for. I just hope you don't get your hopes too far ahead of you. If we aren't able to sell them, I'm not sure we'll be able to commit to more investment."

He cocked his head at her for a moment, the wheels of his mind seeming to grind before her.

"Oh!" he finally said, climbing out of his hole and wiping his hands on his apron. "You must think I mean a monetary success. I only meant to speak of their curing power. You see, the wasting disease in Amoriai is quite bad, and, well … Each pound of woodshear could save ten lives, at least. I think it's just miraculous!"

"Ah," she said, nodding. "Yes, well that *is* quite remarkable. I promise you I'll write."

"Good, good," he said, nodding as if there were no alternative. "Now if you'll only follow me."

He urged her to follow, leading her toward the swamp room, of all places. She trailed along, eager to learn what she could and make her escape.

3

An hour later, Vorseyai was finally heading toward town, a basket over her arm and a sun hat on her head. Ominous clouds were still blowing over the plains, but, for now, brilliant sunlight shimmered off the road. Cicadas sang in the dense thickets lining the road; more or less a perfect summer's day. Now all she needed was for those storms to make good on their threats and bring her some gallant stranger.

She opened her basket, eyeing the block of cheese. It was beginning to sweat in the heat, but at least it was keeping its shape. Of all the retired staff, Yulonrein had been Father's favorite, and she'd hate to bring her anything subpar. Although, Yulonrein could bloody well have everything fresh to her heart's content if she'd live in the pensioners' cottages! Why *was* the woman so stubborn about living in town? It certainly wasn't for the excitement. Yuljeom was prosperous enough, certainly, but even with a dozen house estates in the county, it was still rather sleepy. This deep into the empire, it was a wonder they even got the post some days!

As she walked, the buildings of the town grew larger until she was in the middle of them. Few of the buildings were above two stories, though the place did have a certain charm to it. The dusty dirt road to her estates finally ended in cobblestones — paved by Father, of course — all of it leading to the village green where the temple soared above it all, its giant glass turret casting a kaleidoscope of colors across the grass.

Yulonrein lived just one street over from the inn, but Vorseyai stayed on the main road. If it did rain, it would be better to make her appearance at the temple first and double back. Besides, with all these thoughts of Mother, it seemed she needed the temple's solace rather badly. Visiting the temple was one duty that actually seemed to give something back to her, filling her sails with something a bit stronger than duty or honor could alone.

She stopped to chat with a few villagers, but eventually she made it to the village green, cutting straight across the gravel path. The temple cast a long shadow over the grass, as if the goddess was stretching out to hold the village in her embrace. The golden doors were propped open, and the darkness within seemed to pull at her, inviting her into its stillness.

There was no one in the vestibule, though she heard a few whispers coming from the prayer alcoves. She stopped on the flower-shaped mosaic in the floor, putting her hand on her heart as she looked up at the giant statue of the goddess in the center. She whispered a prayer before opening her eyes and walking toward the statue. She went up to the speaking mirror in its base, placing a gold crown in the pool at her feet. The mirror was about twice her height, rising to the goddess's waist as its silver surface glowed faintly in the lamplight.

She closed her eyes again, glowing with her own golden light as she took on Mother's shape. She'd seen others cry when they looked upon the lost, but she was grateful she'd been able to come until there was no sting left. Now, it simply felt like saying hello, her mother's face looking normal to her again, as if no time had passed.

"I carry you," she said, staring intently into her mother's eyes, "for all of my days, with every beat of my heart."

She glowed again, repeating the ritual with Father's face, looking into the mirror a while longer. Mother would have hated anything more than a moment's glance — a frivolity compared to the tasks she'd set for her daughter — but Father … He wouldn't mind if she stayed all day. She looked into his deep green eyes for a long time, smiling at herself, feeling the urge to hug the figure standing there. Finally, she returned to her own form, bowing before the great mirror and turning to take up her basket again.

As she moved through the atrium, she heard footsteps, as the priest, Child Malpiyeon, emerged from one of the shadowed prayer alcoves. Inwardly she cringed, though she somehow managed to keep the smile plastered to her face.

"Lady Shuwayel," he said, his pointed goatee curling with his gruesome smile. "So lovely to see you back at the temple. We do so appreciate your patronage. If only all in Yuljeom were so devout."

"There is little succor to be found in piety," she said curtly. "I simply come to honor the dead."

"Yes, quite," he said, frowning, reaching into his pocket and running a handkerchief over his glistening forehead. "I am glad you have found peace here in your grief. I only hope the temple can one day bring you joy, too. Perhaps we'll see you in a bridal wreath."

She sniffed, raising an eyebrow. At least he didn't hint at how he'd love to be the one receiving that bridal wreath, as he had before. He seemed to think a two-hundred crown commission and a long shot chance of becoming a bishop could deflect from his unctuous nature. How was it that the glorious love of Essomuai's light withered so in her representatives? She supposed something must be lost when that golden light was melted into coins, though she couldn't blame the goddess. As the Grass House saying went, 'light makes the harvest, but locked doors the rot.'

"I suppose we shall see," she said, pulling her basket back up her arm. "Perhaps next time I can go to town I'll find someone suitable." If only she had a proper chaperone for town this year … not that this bloody weasel of a man needed to know that.

Child Malpiyeon's eyes dimmed at the mention of the capital. He, of course, would be unable to follow the rest of the gentry to Anushai. Still, he found a way to pull the smile back onto his face, the prospects of the last week in Yuljeom clearly still holding some unfounded hope for him.

"Well," he said, "I do wish you all a pleasant season in town. I only hope you'll honor me with a dance at Baron Jullil's before you leave."

Her blood seemed to freeze, but luckily, Mother's training asserted itself, pulling a stock answer from her lips.

"There are always dances enough for the bold, Child Malpiyeon. Perhaps you can ask me tomorrow evening. Now," she added, gesturing to her basket, "I really must be going."

"Yes, well, good evening," he stammered, wringing his hands together as she left. He would, of course, do no such thing as ask her at the ball — it was unseemly for priests to be too forward. It was only in his own domain that he seemed bold enough to pester her. Still, there was something in his eyes she didn't trust, like a liyre cat spotting a mouse. At least the calm and control of Mother's training was always there, ready to turn away the foulest beast.

As she came out of the temple, the storm only looked nearer, choking the horizon in darkness as it pushed its way into town. She crossed the street quickly, very few people with her on the street now that the rain seemed imminent. She walked past the inn, the warm glow of the common room fire making quite the contrast to the howling wind.

She finally reached Yulonrein's house, the little pensioner's flat sitting above a cobbler's. She pulled out her personal key, letting herself in before climbing the stairs to the kitchen. Yulonrein was there on her knees, scrubbing the floors beneath the table.

"Yulonrein!" Vorseyai said, rushing over and picking the woman up.

"Why are you cleaning by yourself, with your bad knee? You know I'd send someone from the house for you."

"Well, my lady," the woman said, looking sheepish as she curtsied, "the knee gets worse during storms, so I wanted to get myself moving beforehand, you see." She wiped her sudsy hands on her apron. "I do apologize for your having to touch my grimy hands though, my lady."

"Nonsense," Vorseyai said, forcing the woman into a chair. "Find me a Grass House woman who can't have a bit of dirt on her hands and I'll have her whipped. Now, you're going to have some cheese while I make more tea, and that's an order. You can't escape me by retiring."

Yulonrein nodded, her face stoic but her eyes shining with pride. You just couldn't replace the loyalty of house acolytes. In this day and age, you simply couldn't find all Grass House servants to run a house anymore, but the ones that still swore their affiliation were priceless.

A few minutes later, as the kettle started to whistle, a sharp crack of thunder tore across the sky. The windows were dusty — she really did need to send someone over to see to them — but the street was nearly dark as night now under that sky. Still, she took the time to carefully pour Yulonrein a cup of tea. The woman had already carefully sliced the cheese, but Vorseyai still opened the preserves for her, unwrapping a few of the biscuits.

"You must sit, dear," Yulonrein said when she was done. "It wouldn't feel right to have such a feast all to myself."

Vorseyai looked out the window again. The thunder seemed to shake the house now as it cracked every few minutes. It was hardly a feast, though the day she was rude to this poor old woman was the day she'd write to the empress to have herself stripped of rank.

"All right, just for a bit," she said, sitting as she took up a biscuit, another flash of lightning brightening the room before plunging them back into darkness.

———

The tea finally drunk, Vorseyai hurried back out of the village as the rain finally began to fall. She felt the first drop strike her head — a giant one, what the farmers liked to call "gods' tears." Dark spots began to dot the road, and before long the skies opened up, the water thrumming down on her. She took her skirt firmly in her hand, marching herself onto the main road. She had taken her gamble, and she would play it out. Even in a rain like this, the time of day was perfect for some gentleman to be traveling east from Sheolden. She only had to make sure she didn't look like a drowned rat when they arrived …

She walked on, occasionally lifting her glove to wipe her brow, careful not to upset the waves still somehow holding in her hair. When she was halfway back to Borimol, she nearly leapt for joy as she spotted a dark shape on the horizon moving quickly through the rain. She pulled off to the side, raising herself up as she glowed with golden light, the rain suddenly gone from her hair and dress. It wouldn't last, of course — a new shape couldn't make the clouds part, after all — but if she looked even a hair more elegant when her help arrived, it would all be to the good.

She squinted through the mist, trying to make out the carriage. She could tell it was a good one, the dark paneling keeping a bit of its shine despite the rain, though she couldn't make out a crest. She knew all of the carriages in the county, of course, thanks to Mother, but it didn't matter much at this point. Any ride would be welcome in the rain, even if it wasn't a promising prospect. If it was an old bachelor like the Earl, she would gratefully take a ride, and if it was someone more … engaging, she would smile all the wider.

Finally, the carriage reached her. The driver wore a wide-brimmed top hat, and he called to the horses, easing them to a stop. She glanced eagerly at the windows, but the curtains were drawn. As a matter of fact, they looked awfully familiar …

"You're lucky I found you when I did!" the driver called out, crawling down from the box. She did her best not to scowl, turning to find Mr. Seoyaln tipping his hat to her. Of course, her own bloody carriage would rescue her from the storm.

"Mr. Seoyaln," she said, keeping her shoulders straight as she moved toward the carriage. "What on Wellonai compelled you to come out in this?"

"Why you, of course," he said, holding the door open for her. "I didn't see you with an umbrella when you left the manor, and those clouds looked absolutely dreadful." He glanced up at the sky, squinting in the rain. "And I suppose they were at that."

"Quite," she said, taking his hand and stepping into the carriage. She forced herself to smile at him as he shut the door. It wasn't as though a man like him would understand the intricacies of courtship. Still, as soon as she was sealed in the darkness of the carriage, her scowl returned. Too gallant by half, indeed!

4

Vorseyai winced, Eserrion's needle nicking her shoulder again as she worked on her dress.

"Don't squirm, my lady," Eserrion said, clicking her tongue. "Serves you right for getting soaked last night. I'll never understand why her ladyship taught you to do that, rest her soul."

Vorseyai resisted the urge to roll her eyes. Still, it felt good to be chided. Besides, a bit of poking was nothing compared to how good it felt to shed her mourning clothes.

She looked at herself in the mirror and smiled, taking in the green satin spilling from her shoulders. It was fitting, actually, to wear one of Mother's dresses on her first night back out, even it did need substantial alterations — especially in the bust. She'd never understand how her figure could be so different from Mother's; it was almost as if she'd inherited all of the Grass House blood and none of the Stone.

"If you don't mind my saying, my lady, it's good to see you smile." Their eyes met in the mirror, Eserrion's smile even wider than her own. "I'm so very excited to see you dance tonight."

With Mother gone, she'd need a chaperone, and Eserrion had been more than happy to oblige. She'd need someone more suitable if she was going to make it to town this season, but it *was* a pleasure to bring the woman to the local balls. She'd supposedly trained in one of the great manors in the capital, though you'd think she'd never been in society before, the way her eyes lit up at some local lord's ballroom.

"I hope to see you dancing myself," Vorseyai said, raising an eyebrow. "That valet at Endoron is always eyeing you. Perhaps you can convince him to neglect his duties for a song or two."

Eserrion scoffed, shaking her head as she went back to the sewing. She was still a very becoming woman, though for whatever reason she seemed unable to give up the role of the lonely governess. She'd always have a home at Borimol, of course, though she'd far prefer it if the woman found some happiness for herself. Perhaps if Seoyaln was low enough for her …

"My lady," Eserrion said, changing the subject as she always did, "I forgot to ask about the theme tonight. Do you need to shape yourself something, or should we check your mother's costume closet?"

Vorseyai froze, her jaw dropping. How could she have forgotten something so important?!

"Oh dear," she said, biting her lip. "It's a house ball, Eserrion. I'm not permitted to shape a thing."

Eserrion's eyes shot toward the clock on the mantel.

"We might just have time, my lady," she said, leaning in as she quickly finished the sewing, somehow avoiding any more pricks from the needle now that it was urgent. "What time is Lady Cullesil coming to fetch us?"

"At half past," Vorseyai said, looking nervously at the clock herself.

"The gardens!" Eserrion cried out. "Let's go see if Mr. Seoyaln can't lend us a plant. Pinning something to your shoulder might be the best we can do on short notice. At least your ladyship is from Grass House; I'd hate to be digging in the dirt before a ball."

Vorseyai's mouth formed a thin line. Another 'favor' from Seoyaln after yesterday's little rescue? It was almost too much to bear.

"Bah!" she puffed, throwing her hands up as she stood. They were her gardens, after all. "We might as well. Come," she said, beckoning for Eserrion to follow. "We don't have much time."

Vorseyai burst from the house, Eserrion at her heels, walking quickly toward the greenhouse. Or as quickly as one could in a sea of silk … She must have looked quite the fearsome creature flying through the house like that, though she hadn't stopped to ask any of the staff their opinions on her foolishness. Thankfully, she saw the flicker of candlelight through the glass, though that would mean facing Mr. Seoyaln.

She'd heard from the staff he liked to do his record keeping in the greenhouse at night. What a bother of a man! Even though Father was still alive when he came to Borimol, it had fallen on her to find Seoyaln a cottage to use as an office. She'd been forced to shuffle several servants around, and as thanks, he just went and started doing his paperwork on a stool beside the plants!

As they shuffled toward the entrance — Eserrion still trying in vain to carry her train — she spotted a pair of garden shears. *Perfect!* she thought, taking them up like a green-thumbed warrior as she pushed her way into the greenhouse. As expected, Seoyaln was sitting on a stool, an overturned barrel beside him covered in papers. He looked up from his accounting, his tiny spectacles making him look like a mole, albeit a more handsome one than what they had in the gardens.

"Vorseyai," he stammered, jumping to his feet. She didn't slow, pushing past him.

"I've come for a flower for my dress," she said over her shoulder, "and I'll not have you keeping me from my own plants."

Mr. Seoyaln began to chuckle. She whipped her head around, finding him standing as he closed his book.

"Certainly not," he said, pulling on his coat. "I was only afraid you'd come here with some … er … murderous intent for your father's work." He gave her a short bow. "The plants are, of course, ever yours to use, and it'd be an honor to help you pick one."

"Very well," she said, gently laying down the garden shears in a planter as she tried to resume her dignity. He led the way, taking her toward the dry room. He'd looked almost courageous there for a moment, facing her down in the candlelight, but as they wove through the plants he began to mutter to himself again. Still, he seemed more a tailor than a botanist this time, his eyes continually flicking back toward her as he appraised her dress.

"I presume you'd like something for your shoulder?" he asked.

Vorseyai shared a look with Eserrion, the older woman's eyebrows arching.

"Why, yes," she said, holding back her mirth. A tailor indeed!

"I think you're in luck," he said, holding the door for her into the dry room. "I have a specimen that only blooms at night. I've been leaving a window open, hoping to bring the bats in and I think—"

"Mr. Seoyaln," she said, stopping in her tracks, "did you say bats?"

"Hmm?" he asked. "Oh, yes, they're actually as important as bees for pollination, depending on the region. In fact in the northwest of Relimora, near the Void, there's one type—"

She stopped listening, suddenly knowing exactly what he was pointing to. There, in the middle of the room, was a gigantic flower, the color of moonlight. It was shaped like a lily, its petals tipped toward the night air as if waiting to capture some dream drifting on the wind.

"It's gorgeous," she whispered stepping toward it. She wasn't sure she'd ever forget that bit about the bats, but it would be worth it to wear such a beauty on her shoulder!

"I thought you'd like it," Seoyaln said, passing her with a stepping stool in hand. He climbed up with a much smaller pair of shears, carefully snipping the flower at its base. He held it reverently, as if it were a child, turning and handing it to her.

"I think that will do very nicely, my lady," Eserrion said, her eyes wide. "Very nicely indeed."

Just then, there was a knock on the door to the dry room. Oeurelai stuck his head in, looking sheepish as he tried to duck his height through the low greenhouse doorway.

"Excuse me, my lady," he said, stepping all the way through so he could bow properly. "Lady Cullesil is here for the ball. She insisted we send for you at once."

Eserrion grumbled under her breath. Vorseyai would need to break her of that habit. She'd known them both since they were in diapers, but she shouldn't make it a habit to talk about women of rank, even if Cullesil could be rather … impulsive.

"Very well," Vorseyai said. "If you'll have her wait in the drawing room, Oeurelai, I should only be a moment."

The footman nodded his way out, and she turned back to Eserrion, lowering her shoulder so the woman could pin the flower in place.

As Vorseyai approached the sitting room, she could already hear Cullesil badgering the butler. Nothing ill-natured, mind you, though the woman was a tempest — and yet, she loved her for it.

"You simply must put the sugar in *before* you pour the whiskey," Cullesil said through the door. "It's how everyone is doing it in the capital."

Oeurelai was waiting on the outside of the drawing room, and he bowed, moving to open the door as he announced her.

"The Lady Vorseyai Shuwayel," he said somberly.

"Enough with all that," Cullesil said, pushing her way to Vorseyai and grabbing her in a firm embrace. The two women couldn't have been less alike in appearance. For all that Vorseyai was willowy and tall, Cullesil was of Earth House stock — even though her mother had married in from River House — and she was built like a steam kettle, her dimpled cheeks the picture of cuteness along with her curling black hair.

"I thought you'd gotten cold feet or something," Cullesil said, pulling away, though she paused as her eyes lit up. "Well," she added, carefully touching the flower on Vorseyai's shoulder, "I see I stand corrected. This will make you the talk of the ball."

"And you?" Vorseyai asked, appraising her. She wore a midnight blue dress with white gloves. "Where's your house memorabilia?"

Cullesil held up a finger, spinning around to show the back of her dress. While the front was entirely of silk, the back was open, held together by a criss-cross of rope.

"Is this … mast rigging?" Vorseyai asked, running a finger along it.

"Impressive, no?" Cullesil asked, turning back around. "Came from one of my uncle's ships. I figured no one would hold it against me if I represented River instead of Earth for one night."

Vorseyai nodded. It *was* impressive. She'd been too scattered to think of something herself, of course, but at least the flower would keep her from being embarrassed. Baron Jullil was a bit of a blowhard, and it would hardly be worth attending if he ended up heckling her all night for lack of a costume.

"Come," Cullesil said, dragging her toward the settee, "Merishail is learning how to make a capital drink, and I think it best we discuss our options at the ball tonight before we head over."

"Don't let her bully you, Merishail," Vorseyai said, smiling at the butler. "A terinal is perfectly fine for me."

"Of course, my lady," he said, nodding with the juniper spirits already in hand.

"So," Vorseyai said, leaning back as she raised an eyebrow, "what has you in such a tizzy?"

Cullesil really was such an odd creature. She loved the hunt of society balls more than anyone she'd ever met, and yet she seemed to only have eyes for the Earl. He would surely marry her, old as he was, if she gave him the slightest of hints, though she seemed content to play the fool. Did she hope to gain some grander promise from him? She only hoped her friend didn't break her own heart. As Mother had liked to say, "only play games with things you don't mind breaking."

"You really do think you're above it all, don't you?" Cullesil asked, rolling her eyes. "Well, you're lucky you have me. If you cared to listen to anyone other than that greenhouse boy of yours, you'd know we have someone truly special coming our way tonight."

Vorseyai opened her mouth at that, but Merishail approached, handing her a drink. *Her greenhouse boy*? Whatever was that supposed to mean?! She took a sip of her drink, forcing Cullesil to wait even though she looked like she might bounce off the settee. Luckily, the terinal was perfect. The lemons had only recently ripened in the garden, and there was just the right hint of sweetness. She swallowed, carefully patting her lips with a napkin. *Exquisite.*

"Well?" Cullesil asked, batting her on the arm. "Don't you care?"

"Very well," Vorseyai said, grinning. "Please, tell me everything you know."

"Well," she said, raising her shoulders, "I have it on good authority from Lady Lewelyin that we have a duke joining us tonight."

Vorseyai looked up from her drink, her eyes widening.

"See?" Cullesil said, raising her eyebrows. "I knew you liked the hunt. You just don't care for the game around here."

"Did you get the name of the duke in question?" Vorseyai asked, her mind already whirring through Mother's lists.

"I'd never heard the name before, *Celanren* or something. He's Fire House, though; I did check that much."

Celanren …

"Cullesil," Vorseyai said, putting her drink down. "He's the wealthiest man in the capital."

"Really?" Cullesil asked, blinking. "But … but Fire men are good for nothing, always in their dramas and whatnot. Whatever industry could his people possibly have?"

"It's textiles or something," Vorseyai said, holding her chin. She closed her eyes, trying to summon the notes. Cullesil seemed impressed, but Mother would have known it all immediately. It seemed her time in the country really had dulled her senses this season. "His father owned the Grand Theatre or something and starting selling curtains after some countess asked about the one on stage."

"Why, that's absurd," Cullesil said, giggling. "I wonder if he's handsome."

"Would he truly be of Fire House if he weren't?" Vorseyai asked. Perhaps she was better than generalizing by house affiliation, but she'd met few exceptions to that particular rule thus far.

"He could always play the villain," Cullesil said, and the two of them started giggling like schoolgirls again. Just then, the door opened, Eserrion appearing beside Ourelai. She had her own flower pinned to her dress, no doubt procured by Mr. Seoyaln.

"I do so hate to interrupt, my ladies," the older woman said, curtseying — albeit while somehow still looking down her nose at Cullesil — "though I do believe you asked me to fetch the coach at half past."

"Well," Vorseyai said, standing. "I suppose it's time we see this duke for ourselves."

They filed out of the room, Cullesil swaying in her slippers as if the dancing had already begun.

5

Before long, they were past the village heading east toward Baron Jullil's estates. The night was surprisingly breezy for the summer, and Vorseyai could hardly make out the rolling of the wagon wheels above the wind. At least the carriage looked halfway decent again ... Mr. Seoyaln — who was riding up front with the *actual* driver, Jeotolm — had done a number on the siding driving it through the mud the day before.

Cullesil was chattering away about all the other expected guests, but she herself had no interest, focusing her mind like a warrior before battle. *A duke.* This was the kind of opportunity Mother had spent a lifetime preparing her for. Sure, there were plenty of dukes at the balls in town during the season, but those balls were choking with beautiful women well above her station, all but cutting off her path to victory.

This battle, however, would be on her own terms. She was the highest born woman in the county, and she wasn't flattering herself by admitting she was the most beautiful, either. A soldier ought to know how sharp his blade was, after all. And as Mother always said, "when a man is in the forest, you must be the tiger."

"You aren't listening to a thing I'm saying, are you?" Cullesil asked, chuckling.

"What?" she asked, blinking in the dim light of the carriage. She looked to Eserrion, where she only received more raised eyebrows.

"I was *saying*," Cullesil said pointedly, "you must be dreaming about the duke. And I see I was right."

"Nonsense," Vorseyai said, waving a hand. "Best not to count your trees while they're still seeds."

"Well," Eserrion said, shifting her shawl on her shoulders, "I think it would only be fitting for you, my lady. You are an incredible catch, if I do say so myself, and it would be much in this duke's favor if he knows quality when he sees it."

"You have to say that," Vorseyai said, smiling as she patted the woman's arm. "You educated me, after all. It'll look badly for you if I prove to be a disgrace."

"Bah," Eserrion said, batting her hand away. "The day you're a disgrace is the day I work for Shadow House, my lady."

Just then, Jeotolm rapped on the roof of the carriage. Trained well by Mother, he was signaling that they were within sight of Baron Jullil's manor, just enough time to ensure their hair and makeup were satisfactory. Even if they'd only just left their own estates behind, a lady simply must be warned about such things. Still, after so much time at home, the excitement got the better of her, and she found herself forsaking her hair to look out the window.

Across the fields, the manor was lit up like a feast day, lanterns shining all across the stonework. She could see other carriages pulling around the circle drive, though the rest of the house was hidden behind a wall of pines. Still, the baron had an exquisite ballroom, made all of glass, and she could tell where it was by the way the mirrored lamps lit the sky around the house in a haze. Whatever came of the duke, this would be a fabulous ball.

The moment Jeotolm had the door open, she sprang from her seat, barely waiting for his hand to help her down. It felt like she'd spent a century in mourning, and it was high time to honor Mother with every skill she'd ever taught her. She moved up the drive, arm in arm with Cullesil as Eserrion trailed behind — though still close enough to be a proper chaperone. Still, if she could have just one season, maybe she'd finally have a marriage bracelet on her wrist, the days of chaperones far behind her.

———

Unfortunately, like most balls, the excitement didn't take long to wear off, especially a house ball … Vorseyai sat at a round table, dully poking at her dinner while the others with Grass affiliations chatted. Sitting in mourning, dreaming of what lay over the horizon, it had been easy to forget what the local balls were really like, which was to say, rather dreadful — at least until the dancing started. Still, she supposed this was her profession, after a fashion, and just like a baker, she couldn't only bake the loaves she loved.

She glanced at Mr. Seoyaln sitting across from her, chatting with Baron Jullil's cousin, Lord Heshan, who was in from the capital. What of Seoyaln's profession? Did he ever lose his fervor for the plants? Was there some task in the greenhouse he dreaded, or some species he abhorred? He would likely think her silly, prattling on about nettles when she should be grateful for her roses. Still, there was only so much sitting in the woods one could do before the hunt became rather dull.

At least from where she sat, she could see the renowned duke, his red coat somehow brighter than all the others gathered at the Fire House table. She hadn't found an opportunity to be introduced earlier, but even from across the room, she could tell how handsome he was. Even sitting down he was a head taller than everyone else, and his jawline looked like it could cut the pheasant on his plate. He said something and the whole table laughed, the merry sound carrying to her across the room.

She would only have a few minutes to reach him. At a house ball, the moment the desserts were out, the band would start to play, and if she didn't catch him by the wine table she might never. Sure, she'd probably pass him in the dancing, but the arrangements at these things were so opaque that it would be nearly impossible to predict how long she might have his hand.

"Say, Vorseyai," Seoyaln said, stealing her attention. "Lord Heshan here says he used to own an apothecary in the city, and he has a few contacts who might make use of your father's plants. If it's not too forward of me, I'd love to have him come by the greenhouse before he goes back to town."

She put on her best smile. Heshan was harmless, of course, but "looking at the greenhouse" would almost certainly turn into a full afternoon of dreadful tea conversation. Still, there was little choice when one was the cousin of a baron. Until she could get Seoyaln to mind his own business, she would have no choice but to take whatever blew in on the wind.

"Why, that would be a delight," she said, nodding. "I can't promise you'll find anything of use. Father's tastes were rather … eclectic, but you're welcome to take a crate of whatever you'd like. Why don't you come tomorrow or the next?"

"I wouldn't be so sure," Heshan said, smiling back. He was a small man, his head barely coming to Seoyaln's shoulder, but he did look very kindly when he smiled, his white mustache curving around his dimples. "Just from the things he's told me so far, I think you could very near run a hospital of your own, my lady."

"Well," she said, "if it's of use I'm more than happy to be proven wrong. Tell me, Lord Heshan, how are things in town? As you know, I've been in mourning, and I've been out of the capital far too long."

The old man bowed his head, putting one hand on his chest.

"My sincerest condolences," he said. "Your mother was a marvelous woman. But the city … I suppose it's bustling as ever, though I have found it most refreshing to pass some time out here in the country with you all this summer. With the war on, I'm afraid we're choking with refugees — all the more reason to get those medicines, of course."

Must everything go back to plants with these bloody men?! Thankfully, Seoyaln butted in, diverting Lord Heshan with his thoughts on some other useless herb. She'd learned basically nothing useful about the goings-on in town, and had invited the man to tea to boot! Perhaps it wasn't too late to find a suitable invitation for the season and see for herself …

She was about to begin another idle conversation with Lady Wulyen when she spotted a footman approaching with the dessert. She nearly fell out of her seat as she looked behind her, finding the butler at the wine table, uncorking a few bottles as he prepared to pour. Such an odd tradition, having lords and ladies select their own vintage. Only a magpie like Jullil would enjoy showing off his wine so much, when most of the grapes came from her own lands! Still, she'd forgive the man anything if it gave her a chance to mingle with the duke.

The rest of the ballroom seemed to catch the cue at the same time she did, every table bursting with activity as guests tried to shed their house affiliations for the few moments they were able. The footman arrived at their table—the raspberry tortes looked surprisingly good—but she had far grander aspirations than stuffing herself with sweets.

"I dare say I'll go have a look at the wine," she said to no one in particular, standing from her chair. "Would anyone like a glass?"

Lord Heshan raised a finger and she nodded, turning away from the table with a smile.

Her heart nearly skipped a beat as the Fire House table also broke up, the duke blessedly moving toward the wine with another man in a red coat. She moved up behind them, just catching the tail end of what the duke was saying.

"—not that I expected much, even with a Fire affiliation. Jullil's a good enough chap, but this really is a backwater."

She felt her neck grow hot at that, but forced herself to swallow her anger. She'd decided long ago to simply pity anyone who failed to see the beauty in Yuljeom. Besides, as Mother had often told her, among the gentry what was arrogant for a count was simply factual for a duke, and if he really had eighty thousand a year he could say what he liked about Yuljeom. Even if he never wanted to visit, she could run her own estates for a hundred lifetimes on that.

"Lord Celanren," she said, curtseying as he turned toward her. "I dare say you were simply at the wrong table. How could the Fire House be anything but dull out here away from the theatres?"

He grinned — or perhaps one would call it a smirk, though it did little to blunt how handsome his face was.

"And which house would you suggest, Lady …?"

"Shuwayel," she said, inclining her head. "Perhaps my own Grass House would have something to offer. This wine, for example, was grown on my estates. What was it the Great Zhulyom said? 'Without wine, the moon would simply be another lantern.'"

"Well," he said, his smile deepening into something more sincere and far more handsome. "I never thought I'd hear a Grass House woman quoting from the stage."

His companion had turned to the wine table, but returned, handing each of them a wine flute. She nodded her thanks, turning back to the duke.

"You never know which hive has the honey, Lord Celanren. Perhaps I'll see you at the dancing."

With that, she turned away, gliding over the floor toward where Cullesil was speaking with the Earl. She hadn't remembered to get a glass for Lord Heshan, but the old man would just have to make do. Hopefully she'd managed to thread the needle with the duke, at least. Mother always said to hint at the color of the flower without giving away its fragrance. With luck, a man like him would actually know the play that last line was from, and if not, at least it wasn't too forward a double entendre …

As she approached the others, Cullesil grabbed her shoulder, leaning in.

"I don't know what you did," she whispered, "but the duke is *watching* you."

She didn't turn around, simply arching her eyebrows as she turned toward the Earl.

"Lord Porsulair," she said, touching his arm, "however do you do? Lady Cullesil was just telling me of the new statuary garden you're building. I'd love to see it when it's complete."

Cullesil blushed, but the Earl's eyes lit up. Perhaps her friend really didn't want to marry the man, but a harmless comment like that certainly couldn't hurt. Although, if she didn't like the man, she wished she'd just come out and say it already! She could do far worse than the Earl. He was old, but he was rich and kind, a particularly rare combination in the empire.

Lord Porsulair opened his mouth to describe the garden in question when she cut him off.

"I'm sorry," Vorseyai said hastily, "before I forget — it seems Mr. Seoyaln may be having Lord Heshan over to see the greenhouse in the next day or so. Would you two mind coming and making a party of it?"

"I'd be honored," the Earl said, inclining his head. "Lady Cullesil, I don't suppose you'd allow me to escort you? Your estates are right on my way to Borimol."

She could be seeing things, but Cullesil's eyes seemed to sparkle just a bit — or had she worn that eyeshadow again? Still, she bowed her head as if to a king.

"The honor would be mine, my lord," she said, touching the Earl's arm.

"Well, it's decided then," Vorseyai said, glancing over at where Seoyaln was still gesticulating to Lord Heshan about plants. "I'll let you know as soon as the day is decided, but I wouldn't be surprised if Seoyaln already has it fixed."

The three of them spent the rest of dessert chatting, until as if on cue — and possibly quite literally at that — the band began to play. The very house itself seemed to dance, the servants rushing about as they picked up silverware and turned the lamps toward the center of the room. Anyone still seated began to stand, abandoning what was left of their dessert as they floated to the dance floor.

Like all house balls, the first dance would be an *essom'tiluw*. It was a dreaded dance — and looked nothing like Essomuai's flower, in her opinion — but at least now that she was the highest ranking Grass House member in the county she could stand in the center and keep her eyes on the duke.

One member from each of the ten houses joined hands in the middle of the dance floor, raising their arms in the air. Given the house order, she ended up between Shadow and Sky, Lord Porsulair and Lady Duyellin on either side. As the hosts, Baron Jullil and his wife stood in the center, their backs to each other as they faced outwards. The others guests lined up outside the circle by house affiliation, Mr. Seoyaln inexplicably lined up behind Lady Duyellin.

As the band began to play — a whirling melody of flutes and drums — the guests in the lines linked hands and entered the circle, ducking under the raised arms of the house heads. The lead of each line danced up to the hosts, bowing before they turned their line back, exiting through the next gap to their right. They wove through the holes like that until each line linked into a little circle, spinning through the formation until there were flashes of color everywhere, dresses and suits swirling past at a remarkable rate.

They went on that way until the end of the song, the crowd finishing where they'd begun as they all broke out into claps and cheers, Baron Jullil and his wife taking grand bows in the center. The violins struck another chord, and the circle broke apart, the house heads preparing to pair off with the person opposite them in the circle. As the baron stepped out of the way to lead his wife in the first waltz, she looked up, finding Lord Celanren directly across from her, a wicked-looking grin on his face.

She curtsied, waiting patiently as he crossed the floor, a certain predatory elegance to his smooth stride.

"I see my luck has finally turned," he said, taking her hand and touching it to his forehead as he bowed.

"I dare say you flatter me," she said, curtsying again. "I've been in mourning so long, I'm not sure I'll remember the steps."

"Ah," he said, "my condolences. Though I suppose that means I have the favor of dancing with a baroness."

"I'm surprised you thought our humble county worthy of such reconnaissance."

"One would hardly expect an actor to take the stage without looking at his lines," he said, looking at her as if she were something he might devour. "Come, I'll lead you."

She took his hand, his other falling on her waist as the band began to play. Unfortunately, she really did have to watch her steps, her slippers rushing before her body as her head swam with wine and cologne. The next number was a *deledel*, forcing her to hop from heel to toe as they spun. Mother's admonitions filling her head didn't make it much easier either, with most of her advice relating to how to look elegant, and very little to do with actual dancing.

Still, it was an incredible experience. His arms were powerful against hers, sweeping her along like a boat on a stormy sea. More importantly, when she did manage to glance about her, the others confirmed what a coup having the duke for the first dance was. With the exception of Cullesil — who smiled like an angel — every other woman at the ball was staring daggers, their mothers looking even more dour at their daughters missing such an opportunity.

Near the end of the number, she forced herself to meet the duke's eyes as everything, even the music, fell away.

"So," he said, without missing a step, "what other hives have the best honey in this county?"

"I'm not sure I could say what would suit the tastes of a man with your … experience," she said, doing her best to look cunning despite watching her footwork from the corner of her eye. "You may pity me once you hear it, but a few guests are coming to my estates tomorrow or the next day to tour my greenhouses. At least the wine is sure to be good."

He barked out a laugh, pushing her easily into a spin. When she turned back toward him, his smirk had returned.

"I'm afraid I may not have long," he said. "Business in the capital and all that. But I'm sorry to miss it, especially if the greenhouses here are as … inviting as the residents."

Without time for another word, the dance was over. Lord Celanren bowed again, turning to his next partner, Lady Relikulm, who nearly elbowed her own cousin out of the way in her eagerness. Vorseyai stood there, her lungs burning as she gasped for breath, grateful her hair was still in place.

"You do look as if you've enjoyed yourself thoroughly," Mr. Seoyaln said behind her. She turned, finding him bowing before her. "Not to disappoint, but I believe I'm next in the order. I would be overjoyed if you'd honor me with a dance."

"Oh, why of course," she said, offering him her hand. He smiled, taking her waist gently as if she were one of Father's most valuable plants.

"Thank you," he said. "I suppose it's for the best. If the duke took you for another turn, I think they'd bore holes through you with their eyes."

She blinked in surprise. Mr. Seoyaln of all people noticed such things?

"I hadn't thought you one to take in the frivolity of the ballroom, Mr. Seoyaln," she said, quirking an eyebrow at him.

"I wasn't always privileged enough to spend my time studying plants," he said, chuckling. Just then, the band struck up another chord, this one signaling a much gentler *zhulanden*. Seoyaln moved in time to the music, somehow seeming to position his arms to lessen the strain on her, allowing her to finally catch her breath. He was a surprisingly pleasant dance partner, very nearly more graceful than the duke himself.

She hadn't ever had the opportunity to dance with him before, with Mother always taking her place in the official dance pairings. Now, she'd likely have the duty of dancing with every person of rank in the county by the time she was wed, though Mr. Seoyaln would hardly be the least pleasant of them. He was a man of nearly infinite vexation, true, but in this at least he seemed keen to redeem himself.

She smiled despite herself as she twirled around the room, her curls bouncing to the music. In fact, the night air seemed to glow, like the moment before a transformation when anything was possible. Her mourning was over, she had met the duke, and her freedom was proving decidedly wonderful.

6

The next day, Vorseyai flew through the house, an army of servants behind her. Leaving mourning for your first ball was one thing, but hosting a garden party? It didn't help that Seoyaln and Heshan had picked the very next day, but there still seemed an endless list of things to do. She certainly hoped he was in a similar state watering all the plants. In fact, he probably thought it was actually all about the greenhouse, fool man! Unfortunately, a garden party was never just a garden party, and there was no telling what the men would do once the sun set, wandering the manor in search of a place to smoke their awful cigars.

They passed by two maids who were frantically dusting the chandeliers. One held a ladder while the other perched precariously at the top, her feather duster carefully bobbing through each piece of crystal.

"That will have to do," Vorseyai said, craning her neck upward. "Terin, I want you to start opening the curtains. Take Hulsil." The woman came down the ladder as if it were on fire, curtseying before the pair of them started taking it down. "Oh, and make sure Mr. Seoyaln has enough men sweeping the paving stones!"

As the two women ducked through the nearest doorway, Merishail cleared his throat.

"My lady," he said, gesturing to the ledger in his hand, "if we could quickly pick the wine? If they don't have time to breathe in the decanter, I'm not sure they'll be fit to serve."

"Yes, yes," she said, pointing the other servants toward various corners of the house before turning back to the butler. He held the wine stock up to her like a menu, and her eyes scanned it, trying to make sense of the dozens of vintages. She'd been taught enough about wine to be mildly discerning, but they hadn't touched the stuff since Father, and it felt like reading those bloody Relimoran pictograms!

"Merishail," she said, pinching her forehead. "I dare say I'll need your advice on this one. I'm sorry I'm not at Father's level yet. We need something palatable but not too expensive. By Essomuai's light, it's not like Lord Heshan is a duke."

Merishail smiled deeply.

"It would be a pleasure, my lady," he said, nodding his head. Like all butlers, the man had a head for such things, and nothing seemed to make him happier than a chance to serve Father beyond the grave. Even looking at the ledger upside-down, his fingers immediately went to one of the names halfway down the list.

"Might I suggest the 1275 Nilanzalm, my lady?" he asked. "Someone discerning might find it inferior, but we have several cases, and with this particular vintner, one would hardly find the flavor of any vintage lacking."

"That'll do," she said, nodding as she turned away. "Just bring a whole case. With Lord Heshan coming, I'll need the relief."

She knew Merishail's eyebrows would rise at that — he seemed one of those men who mistakenly thought all the royals gods — but she didn't have time to turn back. She stormed toward the garden, eager to see how the luncheon was coming.

She was still squabbling with Terin about the placement of the cutlery when she heard the gong ring by the front door. She looked up, finding Mr. Seoylan marching across the grass from the greenhouse.

"I suppose that'll be Lord Heshan," he said, nodding to the maids. "Would you mind if I greeted the old chap?"

"Not in the slightest," Vorseyai said through clenched teeth.

What was one more overstepping of his station? Especially if it gave her another moment to prepare. Besides, it was just Lord Heshan, after all.

"Really, Terin," she said, taking a knife and showing her again how to properly place it across the bread dish. "I know how Father liked things, but somehow we'll have to learn to be fashionable. Wouldn't you want to be on the list of staff going back to town someday?"

The woman flushed, curtseying before she hastily gathered up the knives and went about rearranging them again. Just then, she heard a babble of voices, and Merishail opened the back door, all of her guests apparently having arrived at once. Cullesil ran from the others as if they were a barn fire, crossing the grass in a most unladylike manner as she took Vorseyai in an embrace.

"We met the others on the steps," she said, kissing her on the cheek. "Who would have guessed the Earl's carriage could be so fast!"

"It only goes as quickly as the horses," Lord Porsulair said, stepping up and kissing her hand.

Soon, greetings were flying in every direction, with tea and wine being served as they took their places around the table. She had placed herself by Lord Heshan, decidedly the guest of honor, though Mr. Seoyaln had luckily not separated Cullesil and the Earl.

"I daresay Borimol really is the epitome of the imperial countryside," Lord Heshan said, sighing as he looked out at the garden.

"You flatter me, sir," Vorseyai said, raising her glass. "I do believe you've simply been in town too much of late."

"Hardly!" Lord Heshan said. "In fact, did I ever tell you about the summer I spent with Lady Crelineom when I was young? It was absolutely divine—"

He launched into another story, at least taking the pressure off her to manage conversation for the moment. Perhaps it was the group, but suddenly managing the flow of things felt like pulling briars out of wool. Had mourning really made her so rusty?

The door gong rang once more and her eyes pulled away from Lord Heshan.

"Expecting someone else?" he asked, patiently pausing his story.

"I hadn't thought so," she said, patting him on the arm as she stood. "Excuse me; perhaps I'm needed."

No lady truly needed to check her own door if she had servants, but the cousin of a baron wouldn't know that, surely, and one must take any opportunity they had to politely leave a dreary conversation. As she stepped back into the library, Merishail was coming into the room, trailed by…Lord Celanren.

Vorseyai came up short, her eyes widening.

"I see you weren't expecting me," he said, cutting a dashing figure as he bowed slightly — though only what was appropriate for her station, of course. He wore a satin waistcoat of a deep mauve, and the lace at his neck seemed only to make his jawline all the more striking.

"I suppose I thought you'd already left us," she said, curtseying in return. "I'm sure you'll find the tour quite dull, but I suppose even a Fire gentleman must be around plants once in a while."

"I was able to delay my business for a day," he said, that self-satisfied grin coming back to his face. "Though I daresay you're right. Perhaps I can quench my fire in wine before you let me near the greenhouse."

Merishail met her eyes, giving her a look only she would recognize.

"Perhaps, my lady," he said, tilting his head, "I should run to the cellar and fetch the 1033 Aolemen?"

"Excellent idea, Merishail," she said, nodding. "I wouldn't want the duke to think us provincial."

"I don't see how if you'll be quoting Zhulyom all night," the duke said. "Please, show me to the garden, my lady."

She blushed but put on her best smile, ushering him into the garden as Merishail slipped toward the stairwell. It seemed she was in for far more than she'd bargained for, though. As Mother had liked to say: "The game isn't good until you bet all your pieces."

As they stepped out into the garden, the assembled party all looked up, with more than a few eyes widening. The man was like lightning on a sunny day! She carefully steered Lord Celanren toward the Earl. The old man wasn't much for witty conversation, but his station made him worthy enough, and Cullesil would surely take care of the rest. She herself went back to her seat by Lord Heshan. It wouldn't do to be rude, though she wouldn't object to the view either, sitting directly across from the duke.

After another half hour of conversation — during which she barely listened to Lord Heshan — Mr. Seoyaln stood, giving a slight bow.

"My lords and ladies," he said, "if you're comfortably refreshed, I propose we begin the tour." He gestured at the sky. "The sun is at the perfect angle to see the plants, and most of the flowers will be open — except the night flowers, of course."

"Capital idea," Lord Heshan said, raising his glass despite the lack of a toast.

"I daresay I'm curious to see inside" Lord Porsulair said. "Lady Cullesil talks so fondly of the place you'd think it a magical kingdom."

"Yes, well," Vorseyai said, smiling, "she did like to play hide-and-seek in there, though I'll save you the story of the time she fell into the manure trap." She stood, opening her palms. "Please, Mr. Seoyaln, if you would lead the way."

Cullesil shot her a look, but as they all began to trail after Mr. Seoyaln, she heard a decidedly gay conversation between her and the Earl. Perhaps Cullesil didn't have feelings for the man, but she'd be damned if she let her friend's pride keep her from love. Luckily for her, as she took up the rear the duke pulled up beside her, strolling through the grass as if he were already master of Borimol.

"My compliments on the wine," he said, looking about the grounds. "You say the grapes are from your estates? It's far better than the swill Baron Jullil served us."

It was hard to match the duke's conversation, at once polite and scathing. It was like trying to dance to an ever-changing tempo. Still, each bit of witticism seemed a chance to prove herself, and she'd far prefer that to courtly propriety.

"I thank you, Lord Celanren," she said, pointing to one of the vineyards where it crawled along a hillside in the east. "We don't make the wine — most vintners are of River House stock, as I'm sure you know — but I daresay we have some of the finest grapes, and we receive plenty of fascinating vintages in kind. I suppose Baron Jullil tries, but his lands are so very flat."

Their eyes met, a certain satisfaction seeming to push through the duke's smirk.

"Yes, he is rather an upstart isn't he?" he asked. "I suppose I wouldn't be here if I didn't have a contract with the man, though the trip is proving rather more pleasant than I expected."

Just then they all entered the greenhouse, and Mr. Seoyaln began his tour. It consisted mainly of Seoyaln speaking in a loud voice about the plants in each room until Lord Heshan had a question, at which point the two of them would huddle around some bush with a pair of clippers, whispering like children. They went room by room, eventually reaching the forest room where several dozen more ferns had seemed to appear overnight.

"All seems like a bunch of weeds, wouldn't you say?" the duke asked under his breath.

Vorseyai inclined her head.

"Father was a dear," she whispered back, "but they do rather seem to multiply."

"I would politely disagree," Seoyaln said, breaking out of his tour as he met Celanren's eyes. He waved his arm over the plants in the room. "Each one of these plants could save a life," he said. "They're hardly of less value than a play."

Vorseyai glared at Seoyaln. It was one thing to overstep with your mistress, but with her guests?! She opened her mouth to apologize, but the duke, much to his credit, simply nodded, the flash of anger disappearing from his face.

"Very interesting, Mr. Seoyaln," he said carefully. "Don't mind me, I'm but a servant of the stage. Please, continue your tour."

Seoyaln should have been burnt to dust by her withering look, but he actually had the gall to smile! He turned back toward the plants, taking their group toward a giant fig tree Lord Heshan seemed particularly taken with. The duke paused by a group of ferns, giving her an opportunity to slip beside him.

"I do apologize, Lord Celanren," she said. "Mr. Seoyaln has a tendency to be too passionate for his own good."

"Think nothing of it," the duke said, raising a palm. "It's hardly something to duel over. As my father always said, it's best to listen to your carpenters when they tell you the stage is broken. Besides, I'd be ashamed to lose my temper so easily in the presence of a lady."

She curtsied, flashing him her best smile.

"You do me a great honor, then, sir," she said. "It sounds like your father was a wise man."

"Well," Celanren said, chuckling, "he was certainly a rich one. I don't think the empire has come up with a better way to judge a man's wisdom than that."

"Quite," she said, touching his arm before rejoining the group.

Thankfully, there was only so much tour to give, and they eventually made their way back to the garden. Merishail had been hard at work in their absence, and a dessert wine had been brought out to chill alongside the cake. Thankfully, Mrs. Milanbon had decided to use strawberries in the icing, the deep red at least fitting their most distinguished guest. Before long, the servants had everyone well in hand, and the duke did her the favor of carrying the conversation.

"I suppose I've been rather surprised by your county, all in all," the duke said, absently swirling his wine. "I've never been this far east before, but I admit the provincial life has its charms, even as far from the capital as it is."

"Well," Lord Porsulair said, smiling at Vorseyai, "I dare say you've already met the finest people in Yuljeom. Though, it's not all country boredom here: we do have a fair every summer that's quite a spectacle."

"Oh, yes, the fair!" Cullesil said. "It's in only two days, my lord. You really must stay for it."

"I'm afraid not," he said inclining his head. "You know we actors: a single day longer away from the stage and I might just go up in smoke!" The party all laughed at that, though it seemed a more practiced laugh, the kind all dukes received. "But I do so hope you'll all come to town this year. I'll be hosting the first ball since I ascended, and it would be an honor to have you all."

"I have been trying to impress upon Vorseyai the virtues of going to town," Cullesil said with a meaningful look, "but she seems intent to live as if she were still in mourning."

"Really?" the duke said, suddenly seeming very interested. "I think it criminal a baroness would consider abandoning the capital. From what

I hear, Juelei Hall is quite beautiful."

"You flatter me," Vorseyai said, bowing her head — and promising to herself to have strong words with Cullesil. "Still, I'm afraid it's simply out of the question. Without my mother, I simply don't have a suitable chaperone, and poor Eserrion would run herself ragged managing the house on her own with Merishail here."

"Well," the Earl said, smiling at Cullesil, "I suppose this is as good a time as any to extend a warm invitation to Shildulm. Perhaps you and Cullesil could come so I could take you to the balls — with Lady Guyalin, of course."

Vorseyai smiled, though her blood ran cold. Cullesil's aunt, the Lady Guyalin, was a wretched woman, and spending the season in her company would almost certainly ruin any chances she had at chasing the duke. Her mind whirred through a dozen calculations, finally deciding the bet was worth the risk.

"That is very kind of you, Lord Porsulair," she said. "But I couldn't impose on Shildulm, not with my own house so nearby! I suppose Ouerelai should be given his moment in the sun. I'll speak with Merishail about him joining me to open Juelei. That would take some of the load from Eserrion's shoulders and allow her to act as chaperone. What do you say, Cullesil?"

Giving herself away but not seeming to care, Cullesil smiled first at the Earl before turning to Vorseyai.

"I think it sounds delightful," she said. "I was so hoping to finally see a grand ball like yours, Lord Celanren."

"Well, that settles it," the duke said, a surprisingly genuine smile on his face. "It's the seventeenth of Heyalmes. No theme, simply another night in the empire."

"You know, Vorseyai," Mr. Seoyaln said, making the hairs on her neck stand on end, "if you're opening the house, I think I'd like to join you. Lord Heshan and I may actually be able to work out a supply contract with Lady Relangtum for her new hospital."

She took an opportune sip of her wine, giving her a mind a moment to catch up.

"But what of the greenhouses?" she asked. "I couldn't possibly expect Merishail to manage that as well."

"No, no," Seoyaln said, waving a hand, "nothing to worry him in the slightest. I think Mr. Pelot is ready to take over, at least for a short time, anyway. Besides, it'll be worth a bit of wilting if we can save some lives with the kerilt root."

Mr. Pelot, Seoyaln's foreman, seemed like an oaf, but she didn't much care if he burned the greenhouse down as long as she wasn't trifled with in town!

"You really must consider it," Lord Heshan added, nodding vigorously. "And if you'd attend the meeting with Lady Relangtum as well, I'm sure we'd make a success of it."

"Very well," Vorseyai said. "We'll give it a go." It was impossible to deny Lord Heshan, sad kitten of a man that he was. "And as my father's ward, Mr. Seoyaln, you are of course always welcome at Juelei Hall."

"I suppose this means we can go to Lord Cheomkeln's ball as well," Lord Porsulair said, smiling. "He's been writing to me all summer, though I wasn't sure until just this moment if I'd bother with town this year."

"Ah, splendid," the duke said, inclining his head. "I do sometimes find the count's costume balls tiring, but knowing the company will be this good, I suppose I'll have to accept."

"Yes, well, I should say you already spend enough time in costume as it is," Lord Heshan said, chuckling over his drink.

"Quite," the duke said, not seeming to find the joke in that. "I also do quite a bit of business with Forest House, so it really does serve to attend. At any rate, it will be a good way to kick off the season. His ball is exactly two weeks to the day before mine."

The conversation began to meander again after that, everyone jumping in about what they most missed about the capital, though it hardly seemed to matter what they spoke of any longer. She found herself staring off into the gardens, a wide smile stuck on her face. After all her waiting, she was going back to town. And more importantly, it seemed a lifetime of opportunity was finally aligning.

7

After all the excitement of the duke's visit, the days before the fair had seemed to drag on. There was packing to do, of course — and she oversaw the maids as much as she could — but the prospect of finally returning to town had apparently thrown mud into all the clocks, the minutes barely dragging by. And that was all on top of her usual excitement for the fair itself. Far more fun than any ball, even Mother had found a way to enjoy it, the whole village meeting behind the temple as the sun burned long into the night.

Cullesil came to fetch her just before noon, arriving in her mother's old open-topped phaeton. She wore her white silk hat, waving girlishly as Vorseyai emerged onto the front steps of Borimol. She was wearing Mother's old orange cloche hat herself, as if the sun had perched on her head just for the fair.

"Who do you think will win the Shapewalking competition?" Cullesil asked, her eyes shining as they dashed toward town. "I think Lord Porsulair is competing, and he's really rather good, though you never know who will appear at random from the other side of the county."

"Quite," Vorseyai said, eyeing her friend. That was very near an admission, though Cullesil hardly seemed to notice how transparent she was being. It was like thinking a glass case would hide your knickers!

"Anyway," Cullesil went on, "I asked the cook to make extra cakes for our stand. Lord Porsulair said his cook has taken ill, and it would be a shame if there weren't enough for everyone."

When Cullesil had found the time to inquire about the health of the Earl's cook was beyond her, but she simply nodded.

"I wouldn't worry," Vorseyai said. "Mrs. Milanbon is bringing about a hundred biscuits, so I'm sure there will be enough for everyone."

Honestly, it was barbaric that other counties didn't subsidize festival food for their residents. How could you be cruel enough to charge a farmer two pence for a biscuit when you paid them three pence a month?

There was really no point in being noble if you were going to tighten your fist like a ham.

They reached the village fairly quickly, pulling along the side of the temple where the other carriages were. Unfortunately, Child Malpiyeon was there, waiting like a buzzard to pick off the women of rank as they went into the fair. His eyes lit up as he saw her step down, as if she hadn't rebuked him a week prior. He slid over the grass like a snake, bowing.

"Lady Shuwayel," he said, smiling up at her, "a pleasure to welcome you to the festival." As if he'd made the sun reach the equinox! He didn't even own the grass the bloody temple sat on.

"Child Malpiyeon," she said, nodding as she left him behind, bowed at the waist, as she walked toward the fair. The square of grass behind the temple had been set up like a market, with huge colorful tents arranged in a grid all leading to a stage at the back for the competitions. Cullesil had some quick words with her driver before dashing up behind her.

"My goodness, Vorseyai," she said, chuckling, "you should have seen his face! I could never be so bold with a priest."

"Child Malpiyeon is hardly a priest," she answered with a sniff. "If he doesn't like it, he can forget the gold from Borimol keeping his doors open."

They walked among the stalls until she reached her own, where the cooks were already laying out the strawberry biscuits. Cullesil disappeared to find her own table as Vorseyai stopped, picking up one of the treats. Mostly it was out of respect for the kitchen staff, but as she bit the flaky pastry she nearly gasped, memories pouring in. It felt like she a was a girl again, standing by Father in the gardens, a bright red strawberry in her hand as he urged her to take a bite.

She shook her head, finally remembering to chew as she reached up to wipe an inexplicable tear from her eye.

"Is it … all right, my lady?" Mrs. Milanbon asked, her face grim beneath her chef's hat.

"I should say so," Vorseyai said, smiling. "I think it's altogether too good."

Milanbon bowed, and Vorseyai turned away, carefully popping the second half of the biscuit in her mouth without losing herself in rapture. As she continued down the row, she found Mr. Seoyaln standing behind Father's old booth with the green pinstripes. It seemed rather bothersome to make the staff drag it to town, but at least the thing was getting some use …

He had several children gathered around him, every young person in the village seeming to know him from his demonstrations at the school. Some of the children may well come to work in the greenhouses when they were older, of course, but did he really have to corrupt every generation with his obsession? He was pointing to the leaves of a plant in his hand, a bushy little thing covered in red flowers.

As she turned to go, his hand suddenly began to glow, a miniature blueberry bush appearing where the flowering thing had been before. So the plant *was* his hand! The children all clapped, laughing with delight. He caught her eye, nodding as he smiled. She nodded back, smiling despite herself as she wove back into the crowd. Perhaps with the children gathered about he really was rather more charming than bothersome for once ... She always did try to see what Father had seen in him, though perhaps she ought to try a bit harder.

When she made it to the end of the row, she spotted Cullesil at her family's booth, speaking animatedly to her cook as she pointed toward the Earl on the other end of the fair. What *was* she playing at with him? Did she think a basket of chocolate cakes could make him worship her any more than he already did? Hopefully it wasn't some latent anxiety about her rank ... She may have been from a lesser house, but Cullesil was still of noble birth, was incredibly fetching, and would almost certainly treat the Earl better than anyone else in Anushai.

Determined to help — or meddle, as Cullesil would see it — she wove through the other rows toward Lord Porsulair. She passed by some of the game tents, waving to the man who raffled off the fish every year. There were a few new ones, the most curious of which was a woman who shaped herself into a tree, the children gathered before her trying to throw rings onto her branches.

As she reached the Earl she saw he was just as promised, standing alone at his table without his cook, a paltry pile of tea cakes in front of him. Still, he smiled when he saw her, lifting the hat from his head. Always adamant about dressing up for the children, he had a sort of courtier's outfit on, with frills and ruffles cascading down his arms.

"I hear you're rather in the lurch," she said, looking at his cakes.

"I'm afraid so," he said. "Though you'd be doing me an honor if you took one. I think the others are afraid to leave me without enough."

Having two cakes at the fair wasn't quite in keeping with Mother's training, especially not with the duke to think about. Still, the ones his cook were able to put together did look rather delightful ... She'd made goddess cups, the wide, flute-like pastry horns filled with swirls of cream.

"Well," she said, "I suppose I should oblige you, for the sake of the fair. Besides, I fear Cullesil is planning to bury these lovely cakes with her own."

She grabbed one and took a bite, watching as the Earl's gaze crept unconsciously toward Cullesil's table, his smile widening by several degrees.

"You know," she said, "I thought I might ask your advice."

"Of course," he said, turning back, his warm gaze suddenly reminding her of Father. "I'm not sure of the value of an old man's advice, but I'll surely give it."

"Well, you see, a friend of mine from a few counties over has fallen in love with a very good man. Only, she's from a lesser, Earth-affiliated line, and he's a rather highborn man from Shadow House. I suppose I'm a bit worried about her getting swallowed up in house politics, as new brides are wont to do. Being from Shadow as you are, do you think she ought to worry? I fear she's not a very political creature."

His eyes had drifted to Cullesil again while she spoke, but he looked back at her as she finished, blinking.

"Well," he said, rubbing his hands together, "I don't think she has anything to worry about. Diplomacy isn't all politics, after all. And Shadow House does apparently still have room for dotty old men like me who hardly play the game at all."

"I suppose that's true," she said, nodding. "I don't suppose you have any advice for how my friend might seal the match?"

"I suppose I don't know the particulars," he said, narrowing his eyes, "but no proper gentleman would want his bride to suffer a bad match. Though if he was … *assured* she cares for him, enough to risk some of the more political fears you mentioned, I think he would be a fool not to ask for her hand."

"Very wise, Lord Porsulair," she said, finishing her pastry. "I think I'll tell my friend to do just that. Though, if I may add my own thoughts, I think sometimes such assurances often come in forms we don't expect."

Just then, Cullesil barged over, dragging a struggling cook behind her, his arms laden with cakes. She smiled at the Earl before pointing to the table, whispering instructions in her cook's ear as he laid out the cakes. In the end, they actually looked rather smart, the new cakes arranged so the old ones didn't look like interlopers.

"There," Cullesil said when they were done, "I do think they're rather pleasing to the eye. I hope you don't mind, my lord, I just felt so badly with your cook taking ill. I thought I might share from my kitchens."

"Not at all," Porsulair said, bowing his head. "You've done me a great kindness. In fact, Lady Shuwayel and I were just discussing how much it means to be cared for by one's neighbors. You'll only have to help me eat this bounty. I think you've brought enough cakes for everyone in the village to have a dozen."

Cullesil beamed, chattering away as she stepped closer to the Earl's table. Vorseyai turned away, chuckling as she looked at the stage behind her. The carnival barker — a man named Jhulsen who rode in from Elondin to volunteer — was already pacing the stage, setting up the blocks where contestants would show off their forms. He wore a striped jacket of every different color — clearly a man who knew his patronage came from all houses.

"Vorseyai," Cullesil said, breaking in. "You have to tell Lord Porsulair to compete. He's much too talented to sit out!"

"I do think it rather harsh to disappoint a lady who's so fond of you," Vorseyai said, turning back with a smile. "Why would you deprive the people of your talents, Lord Porsulair?"

"Well, that's high praise, but I'm old enough to need no more trophies on my shelf. I think it time we let some others have a go."

Cullesil pouted, crossing her arms.

"Stop calling yourself old," she said, "not when you look as strong as an ox in that tabard."

Only an Earth House acolyte could think an ox a complimentary comparison, but the Earl still smiled like a schoolboy.

"I dare say you'll still get your chance," Vorseyai said, nodding toward the carnival barker. Jhulsen stepped toward the edge of the stage, raising a cone to his lips.

"Come one, come all!" he shouted, his voice spreading over the fair. "It's time for the annual Yuljeom Contest, where the best Shapewalkers compete for the county crown! Who's brave enough to take one of my five slots?!"

A crowd began to gather in a buzz of conversation as friends jostled each other to raise their hands. Not everyone in the village had enough blood to Shapewalk, but there was usually a healthy mix of commoners in the competition — another vital part of the tradition, of course. A noble who couldn't face defeat at the hands of a talented servant didn't belong in their county, that was for certain. In fact, Lord Porsulair had had a stunning row of close races with his old valet before he died, each man alternating wins for nearly a decade.

"You there!" Jhulsen shouted, pointing to a young farmer with a broad chest. "Looks like your lady there would like to see you try your hand!"

She didn't recognize the man, though Cullesil's lands had more tenant farmers than you could count. The man shrugged, stepping silently onto the stage. Mrs. Luildeyan, the innkeeper, and the postman both volunteered, quickly filling two more of the blocks. Just then, a great gaggle of children wormed their way to the front, pushing Seoyaln before them.

"Please, Mr. Seoyaln?" one begged. "Do it for us, you have to!"

"How about it?!" the carnival barker cried, seizing the moment to point at his next victim. Mr. Seoyaln looked mildly horrified, but he turned to the children, smiling as he took a bow and headed for the stairs.

"All right, folks," Jhulsen said, prowling the stage. "That leaves just one slot for this year's competition. Who'll it be?"

A silence fell over the crowd, all of the obvious candidates already snatched up and the rest worried they'd be next. Jhulsen was a Shapewalker, of course, so he'd be able to pick volunteers from the crowd if they forced his hand.

"The Earl will compete!" Cullesil cried, grabbing Lord Porsulair's hand and throwing it in the air. To his credit, the Earl actually looked pleased, bowing for the crowd that had begun to cheer — likely half in admiration and half in relief. Perhaps her words had gotten to him after all… If only he could follow his victory speech on the stage with a proposal.

"That is a true threat coming to the stage, my good people," Jhulsen said, beckoning for Lord Porsulair to climb the stairs. "For any outlanders visiting us this summer, Lord Porsulair is a man to be reckoned with!"

The Earl meekly raised a hand, taking his position beside Mr. Seoyaln. Those two *were* good representatives of the county nobility. Mr. Seoyaln certainly liked to speak out of turn, but at least he was humble despite his horticultural zealotry. And he did have a way with those children…

"All right, everyone," Jhulsen bellowed, beckoning to the crowd, "now make sure you all come up to the stage. You don't want to miss a bit of the action. All we need now is our judge." He reached into his pocket, reading from a scrap of paper. "Please welcome the county seat, Baroness Vorseyai Shuwayel!"

Vorseyai's eyes widened, though she thankfully kept her mouth from hanging open. She certainly hadn't thought about becoming the county seat during her mourning! The Earl outranked her, of course, but he was just over the county line, and Yuljeom was Grass House land besides. Cullesil's hand was suddenly on her back, pushing her toward the stage. She straightened her shoulders, walking with as much dignity as she could toward the stairs, waving to the cheering crowd as she took the chair set up for her.

"Very well," Jhulsen said, moving to the back of the stage where his own platform rose above the contestant blocks. "Now I'm sure all you fine people remember the rules, but a quick refresher for our contestants. I want to see your best three shapes. Lady Shuwayel will judge you on your speed, smoothness, and originality. You'll have a minute to preen between each, but I want you ready when I ring the bell, all right?"

He took up a golden bell, receiving nods from the five contestants. He raised a mallet, striking it with a ringing tone as the stage began to glow. She stared hard at the figures shining through the light, trying to watch like a judge, albeit it without a single clue what she was meant to be doing. She'd seen the competition nearly two dozen times in her life, of course, but she was never quite sure what differentiated the winners from the losers.

As the contestants reappeared, she quickly scanned the assortment arranged before her. The farmer had become a giant ox, preening with his horns in the air. Animals were common, of course, though this was a particularly large specimen … The postman had taken the form of a … walrus? At least that's what they called those ghastly creatures from the northern cape, right?

The innkeeper had been the quickest, but had appeared as a rather forgettable rendition of the empress — as if she could ever hope to see the woman in the flesh! The Earl, though, was truly impressive. He'd turned into a bell tower, stretching and thinning his form into a tall pole, a bronze bell clanging at the top. Her mouth actually did open a bit at that, but she promptly closed it, nodding as she turned to Mr. Seoyaln. He was, somewhat predictably, a large tree, though the flowers on it were a pleasant pink.

Just then, Jhulsen rang the actual bell, the sound somehow ringing out above Lord Porsulair's as the contestants quickly glowed again. It wasn't part of the rules, but tradition in Yuljeom seemed to dictate that the second round was always in miniature. It seemed designed to save the best for last while also getting the crowd to crane their necks and focus on the forms.

The postman was the first to emerge that time, reappearing as a perfect replica of the carnival barker's hat, tightly woven with intricate rainbow-colored thread. Jhulsen frowned, though, the crowd seemed to like it, clapping as the others returned. Unfortunately, both the farmer and the innkeeper had become grasshoppers, the crowd groaning as they hopped about.

She blinked in surprise at Mr. Seoyaln's shape, the man transforming into a tiny crystal replica of the village temple. There were some whispers from the crowd, Child Malpiyeon's voice unfortunately rising above the rest in admiration. Giving him a run for his money, though, the Earl had turned into a doll that perfectly matched herself, complete with an orange hat and a small wooden chair.

"Horrible luck that!" Jhulsen cried, gesturing to the grasshoppers. "But it's a good round! It'll be close my good people, all down to the final shape. Lady Judge, whenever you're ready!"

She nodded, and he clanged the bell, the golden light sweeping the stage seeming to grow even more powerful. Suddenly, there was a staggering array of shapes on the stage, each more extravagant than the last. The farmer appeared as a large stalagmite, transforming his block along with him into rock. Mrs. Luildeyan became a large, clear bowl, a fish spinning about inside it. The postman wasn't impressive at first glance — taking the form of a giant pile of letters — but as she looked closer, each one had a different colored parchment and stamp.

Mr. Seoyaln's shape wasn't half bad — a giant tortoise with gemstones on its shell — though he had been the quickest to emerge. Still, the Earl's was quite impressive, the man appearing as a tiny storm cloud, snow falling gently beneath it despite the summer heat. She risked a glance at Cullesil, finding her friend's mouth open, one hand clutched tightly to her chest.

With the final clang of the bell, they all turned back into their original forms, watching her as they awaited the judging. She would've liked to pick the farmer, of course, but after the incident with the grasshoppers, it was more or less down to Seoyaln and the Earl. The postmaster had a crown stipend, so she wasn't worried about his feelings, though he *had* given a decent show.

Suddenly, she heard the gaggle of children at the edge of the stage, furiously whispering in support of Mr. Seoyaln. As she looked between her two choices, the Earl met her eyes, giving her a wink, his head just barely inclining toward Seoyaln.

"The winner," she said, standing and taking the large golden cup from Jhulsen, "is Mr. Seoyaln of Borimol." The crowd cheered loudly, Mr. Seoyaln waiting for her on his block while the others left the stage. She marched over to him, handing him the trophy.

"Well done, Mr. Seoyaln," she said, inclining her head.

"Thank you, Vorseyai," he said, smiling. "I'm not certain I had the best performance, but I'm not surprised you put the children first. You are always so kind."

She blinked, tilting her head.

"Yes, well … thank you," she said, frowning as he left the stage, holding his cup high as the children swarmed him. How oddly … encouraging of him. You never could tell if he planned to bite your head off or offer to build you a monument. What a confusing man — as bad as those poisonous flowers in the greenhouse!

She bowed quickly herself before leaving the stage, returning to Lord Porsulair's table. A few villagers came to congratulate him on his performance, thankfully also taking from the mountain of cakes before they left.

"Don't think I missed what you did!" Cullesil cried as the crowd died down, clutching the Earl's arm. "That was horribly gallant, though you did deserve the trophy."

The Earl smiled, looking like the happiest man on Wellonai.

"I daresay the Earl is after a far greater prize," Vorseyai said with satisfaction.

She bid them farewell, wandering the fair to look for her own driver who'd driven the staff over with the biscuits. There was still the horrible business of packing, and they'd be on the road to the capital in only two days. Still, she took her time, strolling between the booths and nodding to villagers she passed. She would miss this place — she always did in town — but if she had any chance of success with the duke … Well, perhaps she would come home with a much bigger prize than a golden cup.

8

A week later — and what felt like a lifetime of living from her valise —
Vorseyai was finally on the last stretch of road before the capital. It was
strange to take the trip without Mother, winding through the same fields
and forests without her chiding advice to fill the carriage. They stayed
at the same respectable inns, ate the same food, and yet she was forced
to be her own mistress. Still, it felt right to stick to the well-worn
itinerary. Mother's wisdom, after all, would be what allowed her to win
the day.

She sat across from Cullesil, their wagon near the middle of the
caravan. They were five wagons in all, the two in the rear holding
luggage and servants — including Eserrion — while the front three were
near to bursting with the blood of Yuljeom. Lord Porsulair's wagon was
in the lead, though she'd failed to convince Cullesil to ride with him.
Lord Heshan was next, joined by Mr. Seoyaln — no doubt spending the
many hours to the capital discussing plants. That left only herself and
Cullesil. It was certainly preferable to ride with a friend than a stranger,
though they may well begin clawing at each other if they didn't escape
the contraption soon.

Cullesil was looking through some letters when she held up two,
fanning them out.

"I suppose I should take it for granted by now," she said, "resourceful
as you are, but thank you for these."

"And they are?" Vorseyai asked, raising an eyebrow.

"Why, only invites to the two most anticipated balls of the season, of
course," she said, folding the letters and whacking her on the knee with
them. "I know we haven't talked about it much — you really can be so
touchy about such things — but I would think it a rather good sign for
your prospects that the duke went to the trouble of securing an invitation
for one such as myself."

Her touchy? Cullesil treated the Earl like a bloody porcelain doll! Still, she smiled in spite of herself. What if she was right? *Was* it a good sign?

"Well," Vorseyai said, smoothing her face, "I wouldn't think Lord Celanren so uncultured as to disregard an invitation he made himself in person."

"Spoken like a true baroness," Cullesil said, rolling her eyes. "Perhaps it happens less when I'm surrounded by your beautiful glow, but such things are done to people of my rank all the time — it's hardly even worth mentioning. An *invite*, on the other hand, is quite like a lightning strike."

"Yes, well," she answered, letting out a sigh, "we shall see. I received an invite myself, of course, but it's not like it came with any other personal letter."

"Bah," Cullesil said, waving a hand, "he's just playing hard to get. Besides, a man like him is absolutely mobbed in the capital. Still, I guarantee he won't be able to forget you, especially after the costume party."

"What kind of mask do you suppose I should make?" Vorseyai asked, biting her lip. "I should think a Fire House duke would have a rather high standard in that regard."

"You mean your mother didn't cover costumes in all those notes?" Cullesil asked, cocking an eyebrow.

Mother most certainly didn't write her lessons down, though Cullesil liked to pretend it was a physical thing — and one she would make you think could fill its own library at that! There was no friend more steadfast, but she just couldn't seem to understand the pressure someone of her rank faced in such things.

"I'm sorry," Cullesil added hastily, noticing her face. "I suppose it's too soon to joke about your mother, dear woman. Still, I wouldn't worry. Lord Cheomkeln isn't even in Fire House, and the duke is sure to find whatever you wear appealing. By the time you reach his ball in two weeks, he'll already be head over heels about you."

"Thank you," she said, squeezing the hand Cullesil offered. "We'll have to see if our luck holds. If I've learned anything about the capital, we'll be crawling through a snake pit to get the prize."

Just then, the driver knocked on the roof of the carriage, announcing their arrival. She pulled the curtain back, blinking in the bright sunlight bouncing off the sea. They were coming from the east, and she could just make out the curve of the port along the water. She leaned to the other side, taking in Mount Seongbelm as it stretched above the palace. This first view of the city always felt a bit like walking over your own grave — the mountain entombing so many of the blood — but it was a good reminder to live while she could, to push with all her might while there was still breath in her lungs.

They turned to the north, crossing over one of the massive stone bridges over the river as thousands of buildings came into view, their smoke threatening to blot out the sky. Still, above it all, the Temple of Essomuai pushed higher, the four canals branching out from its center just visible as cracks of blue in a sea of stone.

"It's incredible," Cullesil said, her face pressed against the window next to hers. "I thought it was amazing as a girl, but I guess it's been so long I've forgotten."

"Perhaps we could take you to the temple," she said with a grin, "see if your flower points to the Earl."

Cullesil turned red, looking out the other window with a huff.

"Yes, well, I suppose we'll have to see if your flower points to a mountain of riches with the duke."

Why *was* she so touchy on the subject? This was the most directly she'd ever hinted at it, and you'd think she'd slapped her. Still, she would actually like to take Cullesil to the temple. Hopefully her joking didn't put her off … They said putting a flower in the temple's fountain could tell your future, with the canal it ended up flowing into telling what kind of life you'd lead. Oddly, when she'd done hers with Mother, the flower had flowed to the west of the city, promising a life spent serving the people, a bit at odds with her current goal … Still, a bigger income *would* mean more servants, more mouths she could feed and shelter.

"I hope you aren't cross," she said, Cullesil's face still determinedly pressed against the glass. "I really would love to take you to the temple. I'll buy you a lily if you'd like."

"Those *are* my favorite," Cullesil said, finally turning back and showing a small smile. She smiled back, taking her friends hand again. Still, she would need to crack this mystery about Lord Porsulair before it killed her and her friend both …

They rolled quickly through the city, passing the consulates and crown offices, ever descending the hills toward the shore. Before long, they were in the neatly cobbled streets of the East End, mansions rearing their heads like ancient gods who'd decided to wake. Still, not everything was as she remembered. There were an awful lot of beggars on the street — southerners by the looks of them, no doubt fleeing the chaos in Alara. The empire was already fit to bursting with refugees, but surely they could do better than letting the poor souls wander the streets?

They finally reached Juelei Hall, the old manor peeking above the neat hedgerows guarding it from the street. A servant was already there, pulling the gate open, allowing the caravan to wrap around the circle drive. She stared up at the tall windows, feeling like she'd been transported in time, before her mourning, as if Father could step through the door at any moment. She stepped out the moment Jeotolm had the door open, moving hastily over the gravel to lay a hand on the ivy-covered wall.

"Hello, old friend," she said, smiling.

She had turned to look for Cullesil when a loud voice called from the street.

"Excuse me!" a man called in a rough accent. "Could I have some help, please?"

She came around the carriage, finding a beggar on the gravel drive. The footman, who still had one hand on the gate, looked as if he'd swallowed his tongue. Everything seemed to slow, her heartbeat pounding in her throat. Jeotolm reached for his whip, and she raised a hand to stop him, but suddenly, Mr. Seoyaln was there, smiling as he shook hands with the man. They talked for a moment, Seoyaln slapping him on the back before handing him a coin, the beggar disappearing beyond the hedge.

Mr. Seoyaln wandered back to the caravan, the tense silence thick enough to cut with a knife.

"Something wrong?" he asked, and everyone jumped back to unloading the carriages, the footman grumbling as he led the Borimol staff into the house with the luggage. Shortly after, Lord Porsulair and Lord Heshan bade them farewell, and it was just Seoyaln, Cullesil, and herself standing on the circle drive.

"Thank you for handling that," Vorseyai said, nodding her head. "Please tell me what you gave him and I'll see you repaid."

"Nonsense," he said, waving a hand. "I could hardly see a better use for it. If it has the empress's face on it, it should do some good, I think."

"How very noble," Cullesil said, though her eyes were still on the street, where the Earl's carriage had just disappeared around the hedgerow.

"Yes, quite," Vorseyai agreed. "Perhaps you might allow me to repay you by showing you the gardens. They're hardly Borimol, but they may just satisfy you for the season."

"That would be lovely," he said. "By the chrysanthemums around the drive, I can already see your father's influence."

"Is that what they are?" she asked, grinning as she left him to follow her into the house.

It truly wasn't Borimol, but Juelei was still a wonder. The moment they entered the great hall, the intricate stonework of the outside gave way to thick brocaded rugs and carefully carved scrollwork wainscoting. Oeurelai was already acting the butler, marching his brigade of maids from room to room to ensure everything had been seen to. She nodded to them, guiding the others through Father's library and onto the terrace.

After two years away — and on her first visit as mistress of the house — the gardens actually did strike her as rather large, at least for the city. The lawn fell away in tiers, holding hundreds of plants while preserving an exquisite view of the sea, waves dotting the horizon as ships darted in and out of port.

"Now that *is* incredible," Mr. Seoyaln said, stepping down the stone steps without waiting for her. Clearly not meaning the view, he knelt by a row of prickly-looking things flanking the flower beds. He turned back, a wide smile on his face.

"I'd always wondered if your father could bear to leave his research when he went to town. This is kerilt, the root we'll be meeting with Lady Relangtum about!"

"Ah yes, of course," Vorseyai said, pinching the bridge of her nose as he turned around again.

Cullesil shook her head smiling.

"Not a word," she whispered sharply. "It's for Father."

Cullesil put her hands up in surrender, and they both turned toward the house, leaving Mr. Seoyaln to find his way through the thickets.

9

It never served to watch the servants too closely as they unwrapped Juelei — the dust made her sneeze, not to mention the questions it raised about what the staff did while they were away. So, she and Cullesil promptly left for the tea shops at Yulemb Square. It was a rather Fire-aligned part of the city being so near to the theatres, but Cullesil would enjoy seeing the who's who of the capital. Besides, Mother's tea shops were all likely horribly out of fashion by now.

Cullesil had made Jeotolm stop for magazines, and she sat on the other side of the carriage, flipping quickly through the pages with more than a few audible gasps.

"What, pray tell, is so shocking?" Vorseyai finally asked, rolling her eyes. "If I didn't know better, I'd think you were reading about a murder."

Cullesil folded the papers with a sigh, slapping them down on the seat beside her with a withering look.

"It all just moves so quickly," she said, poking at the lace trim of her dress. "An hour in the capital and I already feel as if I'm dressed like a grandmother."

Vorseyai bit her tongue, holding back a comment about Lord Porsulair's preference for fashion and choosing a more charitable point of conversation.

"Hardly," she said, "just wear your rank — silk is silk."

Cullesil rolled her eyes.

"Easy for you to say, with *your* body," she said, picking up her magazine again.

They rode for a few more minutes in silence when Cullesil looked up, her eyes wide over the paper.

"Oh dear," she said, turning it to face Vorseyai.

There at the top was an etching of an elegant woman in a frilly dress — her figure decidedly swan-like — next to the words "Lady Nuyeln Takes the Stage … and the Duke?"

"I suppose it doesn't mean anything," Cullesil started rambling as Vorseyai's eyes tore through the article. "They love writing about who's seen with dukes in these bloody gossip pages. It makes sense he'd be seen with actors given his house; it's probably nothing more than a business meeting."

"Well," Vorseyai said, sitting back with a sniff, "one could hardly expect the castle to be unguarded. Besides, she's only the daughter of a baronet."

"Yes, and you're far prettier," Cullesil said firmly, putting the magazine down as if it had burnt her. "Anyone can have a long neck."

They arrived at Yulemb Square, Jeotolm helping them down into a maelstrom of well-to-do pedestrians. The whole place was thrumming with activity, carriages and wagons darting across the cobblestones around the giant golden statue of the empress holding her scepter. Across the square were townhouses and theatres, but the north end was almost entirely tea shops, every other sign some variation of a cup or kettle.

"Oh, Selong Wel's is all the rage," Cullesil said, pointing to a pink sign carved into the shape of a rose.

"I follow the lady's will," Vorseyai said, gesturing for her to lead the way.

What they found inside turned out to be a decidedly cozy tea house, the brightly lit entryway giving way to candles and cushioned alcoves — the fireplaces thankfully unlit. They had pillows and tablecloths of seemingly every color, which was quite sensible, of course. Even if the empress had made all things Fire House de rigueur, you couldn't expect all your customers to forsake the comfort of their own colors.

They elected to lean into Cullesil's house, a liveried maître d' showing them to a plush, sage-green nook about halfway down the left wall. They were each presented with a hand-drawn menu that could comfortably double as a novel in a pinch, with ten thick pages of tea bound in a leather folio.

"Great gods," Cullesil said, "however are you supposed to choose? Just look at all these herbs. Your father would have fainted to see all this!"

There were actually a few things she recognized from the gardens, an apothecary's worth of things you could slip in with your tea for whatever ailed you.

A waiter arrived, and Cullesil ordered a complicated concoction for them both — "for glowing skin" — the man looking impressed as he wrote down the dozen different types of leaves.

Vorseyai leaned back — albeit with her posture still dignified — looking about the room. There were a handful of customers, all of them handsomely dressed, with ornate tea sets before them. She was about to comment to Cullesil on the fineness of the porcelain, when the bell above the door tinkled again.

She turned to find Lady Nuyeln herself walking in, the woman decidedly *more* beautiful in person. The etchings in the papers had somehow failed to capture just how beautifully curved her neck was, or how large her bosom … She was trailed by a half-dozen or so other women, the group not even waiting for the maître d' as they slid into a pink booth that had the look of a throne once Lady Nuyeln was seated at it.

Cullesil was staring with her mouth open, and Vorseyai had to kick her beneath the table before she finally looked away.

"What are the chances?" Cullesil whispered. "This really is a posh place."

Before she could stop herself, Vorseyai was out of her seat, Mother's voice goading her toward the other woman's table. As she took her last step, Lady Nuyeln finally looked up, Vorseyai offering a slight curtsey to reflect their difference in rank.

"Lady Nuyeln," she said smiling. "I hope you don't mind me introducing myself — I'm Baroness Vorseyai Shuwayel. I recognized you from the papers, but I recently had Lord Celanren at my estates in Yuljeom. He absolutely raved about your last performance, and I thought I might come by and make your acquaintance."

The woman had initially narrowed her eyes in annoyance, but at the duke's name she blinked, parting her lips as she met Vorseyai's eyes.

"Well, yes …" she said slowly, "it's a pleasure to meet you. Where did you say your estates were again?"

"Yuljeom," she said, "in the east. I don't suppose you'd know it. Still, I do hope I get to see you on stage while I'm in town. You must be of Fire House, talented as you are. Are you and Lord Celanren cousins?"

"Perhaps only distantly," Lady Nuyeln said with a sniff, looking Vorseyai up and down again. "The season is so very short for those who don't live in town, but you certainly ought to come see the play should you have time."

"I will indeed," Vorseyai said with another curtsey. "I'll leave you to your tea, but I suppose I'll see you again before long — at the duke's ball, perhaps."

The woman blinked again, a pout coming to her lips before she forced a smile. So she hadn't been invited yet … That was a good sign indeed.

"Yes, perhaps," the woman said, inclining her head.

Vorseyai turned on her heel, walking back with her head held high, finding Cullesil surrounded by pastries and a steaming teapot.

"Whatever did you do that for?" Cullesil hissed, gripping her arm as she sat back down.

"As Mother always said, it's better your enemy know you," Vorseyai said under her breath as she took a pastry — ignoring the staring eyes at the other table. "Now I have a pretext to speak to her, and I was nice enough that she won't know I'm a rival until it's too late."

"Well," Cullesil said with a chuckle, "gods forbid I ever cross you."

"Quite," Vorseyai said, squeezing her friend's arm as she bit into her pastry. Just like everything in the capital, it was excellent — the very flavor of summer. But more than anything, it tasted of promise.

10

The next two days passed in a daze, lost in a flurry of preparations for Lord Cheomkeln's ball. She was nervous enough to see Lord Celanren again, but throwing a bloody costume ball on top of it? You may as well tell the ladies they'd be climbing Mount Seongbelm without knowing the weather! Her dress was simple, of course — it may need to be shaped into a new form, anyway — but it seemed she'd wasted a dozen hours sketching and speculating, all without even knowing the theme.

When the night finally arrived, Vorseyai found herself staring up at the grand steps of the mansion, opposite Cullesil on the Earl's arm. She had never seen the house before, but it was certainly spoken of enough about town. The count, Purlais Cheomkeln, was a scion of Forest House and an independently wealthy builder to boot. He was rumored to have massive tracts of forest in the north, but it was this house — built only ten years prior — which had become the envy of the capital.

The front steps swept up two stories before the house was even entered, and at the top of the stairs, a giant clock had been inlaid into the stone above the doorway. She looked nervously at the time, but they were right within their five minute window from the invitation, ensuring they would be anonymous until the judging — at least as far as a mask could truly hide you.

Two footmen let them into a massive entrance hall where rich green carpets ran up matching staircases, all of it lit by what must have been a hundred candles smelling of beeswax and lavender. A butler stood in the center of the room, waiting by a large round table.

"Lord Porsulair, I presume by the time of your arrival?" he asked.

"Quite right," the Earl said with a small smile, "chaperoning the Baroness Vorseyai Shuwayel, and the Lady Cullesil Kesseldion."

"Lord and Lady Cheomkeln extend their warmest welcome," the butler said, bowing.

He stepped aside, revealing three oval-shaped masks laid out on the

58

table, each a perfectly blank porcelain.

"The theme tonight is 'creatures of the forest.' There will be two costume changes after the first and second dances. The winner will be selected after the third round, at which point, open dancing shall commence."

"Well," the Earl said, chuckling as he turned to her and Cullesil, "they certainly are getting more creative in town, aren't they?"

He stepped up to the table and took the mask in the middle, fixing it to his face without a fuss. He started to glow shortly after, his mask reappearing as a furry bear.

"Lord Porsulair," Cullesil giggled, "you look downright monstrous!"

"Good," he said, "not too far from my natural form, then."

"Oh, stop," she said, hitting him lightly on the arm with her fan. She stepped up and took the mask on the right, more carefully tying it on around the curls in her hair. Vorseyai stepped up beside her, doing the same.

"If I may offer a suggestion," the butler said, "the count has hinted that detail will be judged with the most favor."

Detail, was it? She thought of all the animals that filled the forests beside Borimol, a spark finally coming to her. She glowed, returning with the face of a doe. She made sure it was immaculate, carefully stippling white dots across a face full of fine brown hairs.

"That's lovely, Vorseyai," Lord Porsulair said, nodding with approval.

"It really is," Cullesil said, frowning beneath her mask. "I just I hope I can match my dress. I probably shouldn't have worn white."

She glowed for a moment, returning with the face of a snowy owl, complete with ridges on the feathers and a beak over her nose.

"That'll do just splendidly, my dear," Lord Porsulair said. "Now, we'd better be off before the next guests reveal themselves."

The butler bowed again, ushering them toward the ballroom doors.

As the doors opened, they were suddenly transported into a forest. Of some two dozen guests, there were badgers, foxes, and everything in between — though, thankfully, no deer yet. Mirrored lamps on the edges of the room glowed green as they lit an army of potted plants. The ballroom even had a domed fresco, which seemed to have been recently painted, the tops of pine trees exquisitely filling a blue sky.

"Great gods, what won't they do here?" Cullesil whispered, her eyes wide behind her mask.

"It is a bit showy," Vorseyai said, "though I suppose we can't blame the host if they're willing to invite us."

As they moved into the room, she noticed a host's stage where a half dozen people were drinking wine apart from the others. Perhaps the duke was among them? There was one handsome-looking man in a red tunic, though it was hard to be certain without seeing his face.

She turned back toward the others, finding them already over by the wine.

"Well?" she asked Lord Porsulair as she took her own glass. "As our valiant chaperone, who do you feel we should mix with?"

"I dare say it's rather difficult when everyone's anonymous," he said. "Do I introduce myself or simply growl?"

Cullesil laughed at that, touching the Earl's arm, and Vorseyai chuckled, shaking her head. At least one of them was sure to have success tonight.

"Perhaps not the growl," Vorseyai said, "though, I do believe we aren't to introduce ourselves before the competition. I suppose that means we must speak to strangers, at least for now."

Lord Porsulair inclined his head, so she waved for them to follow, leading the way across the dance floor. She aimed for the largest group, where a half dozen people stood in a circle laughing. She scanned their costumes as she approached: a chipmunk, a woodpecker, a pair of wolves, and— She stopped short, suddenly recognizing Lady Nuyeln despite her mask. There was no hiding her figure, her bust on full display as it perched upon her graceful height. Her mask was covered in feathers, an almost disgustingly on the nose swan. As if that were even a forest creature!

She shook her head, forcing herself to approach the group before she was caught lingering at the edges. Still, it was hard not to be shaken. She'd have to compete a good deal better than this woman if she was to be noticed. But how exactly was she to best an actress? They were practically professional Shapewalkers.

"Well, if this isn't a handsome group of creatures," she said, curtseying as she stepped into a small gap in the group. "I suppose I can't introduce myself, but if you'll allow me to join you, I promise I'm a '*dear*.'"

Thankfully, she earned a few chuckles at that, the group heartily welcoming her as they made room for Cullesil and the Earl as well. As they slipped into the conversation, she watched Lady Nuyeln from the corner of her eye. What would Mother say in this situation? She had always said that charm was better than beauty — if a woman knew how to wield it, of course. But how to charm here? The costume changes, perhaps? She wouldn't win on elegance alone, but the butler did say to focus on detail, and it wasn't as if Lady Nuyeln had spent much time in the forest …

As they chatted, more guests continued to arrive, the room filling with all manner of masks. In the end, another dozen guests appeared before a man — presumably Lord Cheomkeln, despite his beaver mask — stepped to the front of the stage, clapping his hands together.

"My dearest guests!" he bellowed, spreading his hands wide, a glass in one hand. "I am your host, Lord Beaver."

The crowd graciously laughed at that — the man had paid for the wine, after all.

"I hope you enjoy the festivities tonight. This theme has a special place in my heart, the forest not only providing my house affiliation, but my livelihood. May we all be grateful for the passions that drive us."

"Hear, hear!" someone in the crowd called back, and the whole ballroom raised their glasses, drinking to the count.

"Now," he said, "it's time for the first dance." He pointed to two long strips of tile inlaid into the marble floor. "Ladies, please line up on the left, and don't worry about finding a partner. Even if you've chosen the most gruesome creature in the forest, you're sure to find a beast to suit you."

As everyone began to scurry to find a position, the valets turned more lamps toward the dance floor, the whole space transforming under a haze of green and gold. The band began to tune as the count walked off stage, the center of each line left open for the hosts.

Vorseyai made sure Cullesil was directly across from the Earl, leaving herself facing a rather handsome-looking wolf. The count announced the first dance — an *eldenshin* — and with a strum of the violin, the men and women were marching toward each other like enemy soldiers. Just before impact, they raised their hands, meeting in the middle as they twirled around, trading places before moving down the line, the dancers flowing like a snake coiling in on itself.

As she reached the end of the line and looped back into the fray, she passed the man from the stage, his red tunic under a boar-shaped mask. He gave her hand an extra squeeze as she passed, her cheeks flushing as she moved on to Lord Cheomkeln. *Had* that been the duke? Her head was still swimming as the song ended, her breast heaving beneath the layers of silk.

"Well!" Lord Cheomkeln said, stepping to the middle of the room, his own chest heaving beneath his cravat. "That was some of the finest dancing I think I've ever seen! But," he added, raising a finger, "don't forget the competition; it's time to take your second form. Please keep the same beast, but really do bring it to life."

He bowed, and the whole room began to glow. Panicking only slightly, Vorseyai clamped her eyes shut, taking the first idea that came to mind as the lightness entered her chest. She focused on her dress, the fabric suddenly rippling with fur as she filled it with the detailed markings of a deer. She even shaped her shoes, turning the slippers to leather as she cleft them into hooves.

Thankfully, as she opened her eyes, she found her idea wasn't wholly unoriginal. A few of the guests had shaped their hats instead, one woman dressed as a peacock now sprouting feathers above her head. She scanned the line of men, finding the boar in the middle, his fearsome tusks suddenly covered in blood.

"Well," Cullesil whispered, her own mask now sporting glowing yellow eyes above her own, "at least you won't have any problems with the poultry."

Vorseyai glanced down the line, finding Lady Nuyeln delightfully uninspiring, her dress now covered in simple white feathers. Still, the woman seemed completely confident, keeping her eyes straight ahead while every other guest sized up the competition.

"Splendid! Splendid!" Lord Cheomkeln said, clapping as he spun around the room, his own suit now complete with a beaver's tail. "I hope you haven't made yourselves too monstrous, though, because it's time for the second dance. Whoever you're across from, please partner up for a *reldinair*."

The count must have a cruel sense of humor, picking a dance like that. It was from the Three Sisters, if she remembered correctly, and the steps were horribly complicated. At least she hadn't added heels to her slippers … She looked up to find the lines had shifted just slightly, Lord Porsulair standing in the place of the wolf. He smiled at her under his mask, raising a silly-looking paw.

"Are you enjoying yourself?" Lord Porsulair asked warmly as they twirled around, though his gaze still flickered about the dance floor in search of his beloved owl.

"It's lovely," she said, smiling. "It is so good of you to chaperone us. Cullesil simply can't stop raving about how kind you are for coming all this way."

"Oh?" he asked innocently, though the sparkle in his eyes gave him away. "Really, it's no trouble. If anything, I should be thanking you for securing us such dazzling invitations."

"Nonsense," Vorseyai said, taking hold of his wrist for the final turn, "if ever there were a scandal, it would be in not inviting the kingdom's greatest Shapewalker to a costume ball."

With that, she spun out from the Earl's hand, extending her arm before gracefully turning back into his arms. He let go, the music ending as the crowd clapped.

"You're a lovely dancer," Vorseyai said, curtseying. "I only hope you'll give Cullesil the pleasure of the next dance."

"I dare say I shall," the Earl said, bowing form the waist as the owl in question skipped toward them across the dance floor.

"You two made quite a sight!" Cullesil said, squeezing the Earl's arm.

"I wouldn't know," Lord Porsulair said, chuckling, "everyone's eyes were on you, my dear."

"Oh, stop!" she said, swatting at him.

She opened her mouth to say more when the count stepped to the center of the room again, the party falling into a hushed silence. Vorseyai ignored his announcement this time, thinking only of her transformation as she closed her eyes. The moment he clapped, she was glowing, weaving an intricate design in her mind. Perhaps it didn't fit the anatomy of a doe, but she forced her mask to form two giant antlers above her head. She made them hollow and covered them with tiny golden pendants to catch the light.

As she opened her eyes, her coup was obvious, most of the eyes in the crowd already turned toward her. As they caught the light, the pendants bathed her in golden light, almost as if she were still transforming. The others were just as impressive — fur and fangs and feathers seemingly tripled since the previous round — though no one seemed to have the ornamentation she did. Even Lord Cheomkeln looked at her, blinking before he collected himself.

"Well," the count said, shaking his head, "I certainly never dreamed of seeing such a majestic array, even with so many titans of the stage in our presence."

She scanned the room for Lady Nuyeln, finding the woman scowling at her now, her sleeves transformed into rather boring looking wings.

"Now," Lord Cheomkeln said extending his arms to either side, "it is time for the judging. Please refresh yourselves and be comfortable. Soon, all will be revealed."

He retreated to his own table on the raised platform, joined by his guests of honor — the presumed duke in the boar's head mask at his side. The room watched in silence until the count turned away, every guest suddenly whispering in groups or dashing for the wine. Luckily, Lord Porsulair wove toward them, a glass already in each hand.

"For you, my dears," he said, nodding for them to take a glass.

"And what about you?" Cullesil said, giving him a sharp look. "That's so like you, thinking nothing of yourself."

She waved away the wine he offered her, disappearing into the crowd to find her own. The Earl chuckled to himself, shaking his head.

"Spirited, isn't she?" he asked.

"If nothing else, she's that," Vorseyai said, smiling. "She'll make a stupendous wife to someone."

"Yes, quite," the Earl said, his eyes unconsciously following her through the crowd.

Finally, the count returned to the front of the stage, his valets turning the mirrored lamps away from the dance floor and onto him.

"What a splendid ball," he said. "I dare say I've never seen such a display of wonderful costumes. Alas, this *is* a competition, and so, my beautiful wife, the Lady Cheomkeln, will announce the winner."

The marchioness was on the side of the stage, where she accepted a roll of parchment from the butler.

"As my husband said, there were so many delightful costumes. But after much deliberation, this year's winner is—" she glanced down at the parchment, pausing for effect "—the forest deer by Baroness Vorseyai Shuwayel of Borimol! Everyone, a round of applause, please."

She was…the winner? The entire crowd seemed to move as one, looking about the room to find her as the clapping finally began. Her neck grew hot, but she remembered to curtsey, waving as the cheers died down.

"Now, please do enjoy yourselves," the count said, waving for his servants to flood the dance floor again, trays in hand. "I demand not a drop of wine be left behind tonight. And remember to save your masks."

He motioned below the stage where a long table had been set up. The guests seemed to take Lord Cheomkeln at his word, many removing their masks to drink the wine more quickly as they placed them in front. Vorseyai turned to take another glass for herself when a footman suddenly appeared at her side.

"My lady," he said, bowing as he gestured toward the raised platform. "If you would do your hosts the honor of a toast."

Lord Cheomkeln and his distinguished guests were standing in a group on the stage, the wine in their glasses shimmering in the candlelight. They had all removed their masks, at last revealing the duke. Their eyes met, the same predatory smile appearing on his face.

"Well," she said, turning to Cullesil as her pulse thumped in her throat, "I suppose we ought to join them."

Cullesil nodded, squeezing the Earl's shoulder as they set off across the dance floor. They made a quick stop to drop off their masks, the hired painter already setting up his easel to capture them. But as they reached the stairs to the stage, the butler appeared on the steps, barring the way.

"I'm sorry, my lady," the butler said, looming over her, "the invitation was only for yourself, I'm afraid. The marchioness must have a regard for rank, visible as she is in her own home."

She blinked in surprise, meeting Lady Cheomkeln's eyes, the other woman looking quickly back toward her friends. Were they really so vain in town as to snub her friend? Cullesil's rank had never once come up in Yuljeom. She was about to open her mouth with a retort — the duke be damned — when Cullesil grabbed her arm.

"It's all right," she whispered, her eyes wide. "Go and join them. You'll bring me with you someday."

She bit her lip, but Cullesil simply winked, turning back toward the Earl and laughing loudly as if the whole thing were a simple misunderstanding. Vorseyai shook her head, turning toward the butler who was already bowing, sweeping out of her way.

"Lady Shuwayel!" the count said, turning to her as if he hadn't just ignored her friend being snubbed. "You really did outdo yourself. I knew you'd be a worthy guest when Lord Celanren suggested your invitation, but he hadn't told me he'd be rigging the game!"

His wife smiled by his side, touching her arm as she offered her congratulations. They chatted for a few minutes — the count apparently vaguely remembering Father — but it wasn't long before a more formidable shape moved into view. She looked up to find the duke stepping toward her, a small, dark-haired woman on his arm. Her heart seemed to skip a beat. The woman was stunning! Had she come all this way and defeated Lady Nuyeln to be disappointed by some fiancée he'd simply 'failed' to mention at Borimol?

"Lady Shuwayel," he said, nodding. He gestured to the angelic woman beside him. "My sister, Lady Shailhun. Her husband is away on naval business, I'm afraid, so she's been saddled with her brother for the evening."

Suddenly, it seemed she could breathe again, a broad smile finally pushing its way onto her face as she took the woman's hand.

"A pleasure," Vorseyai said, going into a half-bow as she squeezed Lady Shailhun's hand. She seemed to recall the name but couldn't remember quite where she ranked by comparison. Not that it mattered, the woman looking back at her with a gaze so icy it could freeze a lake.

"Quite," was all Lady Shailhun said, taking her hand back as she raised it for a fresh glass of wine. Luckily, the duke seemed to have ignored the entire exchange.

"Well," he said, "I never thought a member of Grass House would be so competitive at costumes, of all things."

"I hardly think Fire House invented the things," Vorseyai said with a wink. "I think it's simply you lot who grew so comfortable you couldn't take them off."

He chuckled at that, but against all odds, his sister actually looked back from her surveillance of the dance floor, the slightest of smiles quirking on her lips.

"I wasn't aware you courted clever girls these days, Elindron," she said to her brother, though her eyes never left Vorseyai. Her whole chest began to flush, the implication suddenly seeming to give her away and leave her bare.

"I shouldn't think Lady Shuwayel so crass as to feel 'courted' by a single invitation," the duke said drily, giving his sister a withering look.

"Anyway," he said, looking back at Vorseyai, "it's still refreshing to see something new from your house. I'm afraid I've grown too used to Grass being unbearably … humanitarian. Wasn't it Lord Heshan I saw in Yuljeom trying to procure herbs, or some such thing?"

"Yes, it was," Vorseyai said, nodding her head. "I suppose the plants were a project of my father's, though I shan't complain if they do some good before they dry on the vine."

"Well," Lord Cheomkeln said pushing his way into the conversation with his wife on his arm, "don't forget to profit if you've done all the work, my dear."

That was perhaps the most obvious Forest House statement she'd ever heard in her life, but she simply smiled, inclining her head again. Still, it seemed he thought the lesson only half learned.

"You see," he said, gesturing with his wine, "the empire hasn't stood through virtue alone, my dear. It remains because our forefathers had *drive*. I dare say, magic isn't given to the kind. It is blood, like any other, and it can be spilled or hardened like metal in a forge."

"You sound like a fanatic," Lady Shailhun said, chuckling into her wine, though Vorseyai wasn't quite sure what the joke was.

"I'm merely a pragmatist," Lord Cheomkeln said, raising his glass toward Lady Shailhun as if she hadn't just used him for sport. "Take the conflict in Alara. It's good for business, sure, but we're not there to stroll through the daisies. The empire must be preserved by force."

She had never been one for politics — the papers were a week old in Yuljeom, anyway — but she still felt the pressure to say something. As

Mother always said, "a lady ought not be opinionated, but neither should she be a dullard."

"What say you, Lord Celanren?" she asked, slightly raising her glass in his direction.

"Well," he said, chuckling mirthlessly in an eerily similar way to his sister, "my family hardly has many buyers of silk in the military, but I should say I agree in principle. If the empire is an ax, you may as well cut some wood."

"Quite," she said, though that was hardly a reassuring line of thinking — and it did nearly nothing to illuminate his stance on the war, beyond his opportunism. Still, it seemed to earn her a smile from Lady Cheomkeln.

"Say," Lord Cheomkeln asked, "what of your family, Lady Shuwayel? Do your people have any industry?"

"I suppose we're more traditional," she said, tapping her chin in the way that Mother had taught her to accentuate her dimples. "We still rely mostly on tenancy."

"Ghastly business," Lady Shailhun said, shaking her head. "We have nearly a thousand hectares in Selonglel, but it's hardly worth the trouble. Why wait a whole season for a farmer to grow a bloody pumpkin when you could make the money in a day at the factory?"

Did they have no preoccupation other than their damned riches?! Still, it did confirm her suspicions that the Celanrens were drowning in gold. Perhaps with her to shepherd their better angels …

Just then, the band began to thrum their violins, signaling another song.

"Well," Vorseyai said, curtseying to her hosts, "you have my sincerest thanks for your invitation. I am humbled too by my victory. I hope to see you all on the dance floor."

She received another toast from the four of them before slipping off the stage. As she moved toward Cullesil, she caught the duke watching her out of the corner of her eye. It seemed Mother's advice had done it again. Someone else might have lingered too long on the stage, looking desperate for a dance with the duke, but wolves only chased rabbits in the thicket. If he bloodied his teeth without a promise, he'd have no use for her.

As she turned toward Cullesil, though, she felt a drop in her stomach. She was sitting with Lord Porsulair at their dining table, her makeup looking like it had run in the lamplight, her handkerchief in hand. She rushed over, her dress rustling as she cut through the assembling dance partners.

"I'm so sorry, darling," she said, squeezing Cullesil's shoulder. "It was horrid of them to pull rank on you. I promise that will never be the case with me."

"It's all right," Cullesil said, turning her face up to her and smiling widely. "I'm sure you were a smash up there. Besides, I had someone lovely to console me."

Finally, she noticed Cullesil's hands wrapped up in the Earl's, the gentleman smiling like a child. Her makeup had indeed smeared a bit, but upon closer inspection, it seemed to have dried, the tears apparently long forgotten.

"Yes," Vorseyai said, smiling. "Perhaps it was for the best, after all."

<h1 style="text-align:center">11</h1>

The days slid by after the first ball, the familiar rhythms of town finally easing her back into a stupor of tradition and summer heat. At first, Cullesil's relative lack of experience had made everything seem new. But even after a year away herself, it wasn't long before the torpor of long afternoons took over. They dined with Lord Porsulair nearly every evening, of course, but other than waiting for Lord Celanren's ball, there was little else to do.

Five days out from Lord Celanren's, Vorseyai found herself on the back veranda with Cullesil, the sun baking the tiled roof above them. Mr. Seoyaln was puttering around the garden, but otherwise, the house was quiet, Oeurelai seemingly the only other living thing in the manor as he stepped out to refill their drinks.

"Do you really think that dress will fit me?" Cullesil asked, rolling her head to face her from the chair she was lounging in.

"Trust me," Vorseyai said for the fifteenth time, "I know it's not your usual cut, but what's the point of getting a dress in town if you aren't buying the latest?"

"I suppose," Cullesil answered, taking a sip of her drink. "But I could easily buy three dresses in Yuljeom for the money, and that *color* ... I just don't know!"

"The color is lovely," she said, rolling her eyes. "You said yourself purple is the Earl's favorite."

Cullesil grew quiet at that, but when Vorseyai turned toward her, she was staring into her drink, not a trace of anger on her face. Only a certain ... wistfulness.

"What is it?" she asked. She still felt on eggshells after Cullesil's reaction on their way into town, but after what she'd seen at the ball, surely there must be no room for pretense any longer...

"Well ..." Cullesil began, but she shook her head. "Never mind."

"That's quite enough!" Vorseyai cried out, flying up in her seat. She heard a laugh from Mr. Seoyaln somewhere in the distance but ignored it, lowering her voice to a harsh whisper.

"Now, I know what I saw at the bloody ball. Lord Porsulair worships you, so *what* in the sweet goddess's name is there to be so wishy-washy about?"

Cullesil's eyes widened by half, but after a moment, she actually started to laugh.

"I suppose you're right," she said, shaking her head. She took a deep breath, biting her lip. "Don't be mad, I know I should've come out with it ages ago, but … he proposed to me at the ball."

They locked eyes again, Cullesil's face suddenly shining like the sun as she smiled.

"And?" Vorseyai asked, raising her hands. "What was your answer?"

"Well," Cullesil said, her face suddenly falling again, "you see, I haven't given him one yet."

Vorseyai forced herself to take in a deep breath, anything to keep her from throttling her closest friend in the world.

"I know, I know," Cullesil said, grabbing her hand and squeezing it. "I'm ever so flattered and grateful. I mean, me, a countess! He's simply the loveliest man I've ever met, so noble and kind. But won't everyone think me an *eyulcen*? My father's farms are fine enough, but my rank is hardly anything to blink at."

"Darling," Vorseyai said, taking Cullesil firmly by the shoulder, "you didn't have the benefit of my mother's education, so I'm trying to be patient with you, but that is the most foolish thing I've ever heard in my entire life. The Earl is madly in love with you, and he has every right to be. You will improve your position, true, but you will love him better than anyone in the empire, let alone Yuljeom. If you really feel the same way, I demand you take the carriage to his house this instant and give him your answer."

Finally, Cullesil blinked, as if snapping out of a trance.

"Yes," she said quietly, nodding, "yes, I think you're right."

Vorseyai reached for the bell, but Cullesil was already gone, marching herself toward the carriage house. Vorseyai chuckled, plopping back down in her chair. At least something could be accomplished this summer — and something that had been brewing for three seasons, at that. There was still little assurance her own campaign would be successful, but this felt good.

She lay in the heat again, the afternoon burning away as the sun rolled over the sea. Her drink was disappearing a bit faster than was perhaps respectable in company, but there had to be some benefit to being the lady of the house, no? She had very nearly fallen asleep, drifting with her eyes closed, when she suddenly heard the piano playing in the other room, her eyes fluttering open.

Father, she thought as she recognized the tune, "The Wind in the Flowers." It had been his favorite, one of the only things he ever played during the summer. She shook her head and stood, floating toward the sitting room as if walking in her sleep. She opened the door, about to call out to him when she noticed Mr. Seoyaln at the piano. Her face fell. Of course … Father was gone. She'd only been dreaming.

As her foot creaked on the wood, Seoyaln stopped playing, turning with a bashful look on his face. When had he gotten past her from the garden?

"I do apologize," he said, standing quickly and making a little bow. "I didn't mean to disturb you, you looked so peaceful sleeping on the veranda. I'd just been meaning to play since we arrived."

"Don't mention it," she said, shaking her head as she struggled to push through her daze. "I suppose I hadn't realized you play."

"Since I was a child," he said, smiling. "I really do hope you don't mind. Sometimes I just like to make sure all the hard work my tutors put in hasn't slipped away. I suppose it's like the plants, making sure they've flowered properly."

Mr. Seoyaln with tutors? That was odd enough in its own right, but there weren't many who knew that particular song. She glanced behind him but found no sheet music.

"How do you know that song?" she asked.

"Your father taught me," he said, smiling. "I think it was three summers ago, when you went to town and he stayed at Borimol for the seris crop."

"Well," she said, finally finding the wherewithal to smile, "it is lovely to hear it again. You're welcome to the piano whenever you'd like, of course."

"Thank you, truly," he said, bowing again. "Oh, by the way, don't forget we're meeting Lady Cruseln the day after next for lunch at the Sherolm Inn."

"Certainly," she said, inclining her head. "Now, I'll leave you to it. Please do enjoy the piano."

She turned back to the veranda, just making it to her seat as a tear came to her eye. Suddenly, it seemed as if all her memories had come surging back, the song blowing them in like the summer wind. So many moments with Father bloomed in her mind, though one in particular seemed to shine brighter than the others. It was that last summer, just before he'd died. Mother had gone somewhere to see friends, and it had just been the two of them.

It was the first summer that Father had really seemed comfortable sharing a drink with her, his eyes finally seeming to no longer see a little princess before him. She had somehow needled him into opening the 1150 Halinjaem, and they had sat sipping it in these same chairs, watching the sun as it tilted toward the endless blue of the western sea.

It was honestly hard to know what to say to Father when he was away from his greenhouse. At Borimol, he always seemed to have a thousand ideas spouting from his mouth, each one woven with stories and bits of history, like an oracle divining the will of the gods. But in town, he seemed a different man altogether, as if he didn't know what to do with himself, Mother's estates and the very walls of Juelei Hall seeming a prison to him.

"Do you think you'll join us at Lady Yelomken's?" she remembered asking, clearly desperate if she'd ask Father about a ball, of all things.

"Hmm?" he'd asked, looking up from his drink, the wine bubbling off the sides of the crystal. "Oh, I suppose not. Your mother does hate the way I blather on at those things."

"Well, I should like you there," she'd said, reaching across and squeezing his arm. It wasn't just Mother's habit of parading her around she wanted to avoid. The balls just felt so much more … magical when Father was there. Even the carriage seemed fuller somehow, as if it would take a sudden turn and lead them to a new world.

They had sat in silence for a while longer when Father suddenly turned to face her.

"Do you ever think you'd like something more than balls, darling?" he asked, his eyes seeming sad.

"How do you mean?" she asked. "Of course, I'd like to have a family of my own someday. It would be nice to have children at Borimol again, chasing you through the gardens."

He smiled for a moment, but it seemed to lose the fight against the rest of him, the melancholy returning to his eyes. It was the kind of look he had on the days he locked himself in the library.

"But to what will you dedicate your breaths, daughter?" he asked, looking out at the terrace. "Take the plants, drinking in the sun as they push every ounce of their being into life. You have a choice, to grow, to feed, to become more than the seed you were when you began. Do you understand what I mean?"

He did like to quote poetry at her, but this didn't seem like one of his usual verses.

"I suppose you mean the gardens?" she asked. "Of course, I'll always maintain Borimol, Father, you shouldn't worry about that. I do like the thought of caring for our people. The staff do so love you, after all. At any rate, I shan't neglect my duty, so don't worry about that."

He sighed, leaning back in his chair. Still, he turned back for just a moment, offering her a smile.

"You are ever so sweet, my daughter," he said, looking back out at the sea. "Don't worry too much about the ramblings of an old man. Whatever life you lead, I'm sure it will be a splendorous one. Just … don't let yourself be blinded by it all. Your Mother loves you, gods bless her for that, at least, but there is more to life than being wed. Don't forget, there are many views on the mountain. You always have a choice."

That was all she remembered. She must have turned him to some lighter topic after that, always eager to keep his melancholy from getting the best of him. They may have even had dinner in town that night, just the two of them, each moment terribly precious in those last years of his life. If only he were still here now to see what she'd made of herself. What would he think of her trying her hand at becoming a duchess? If she succeeded, she could grow Borimol into something her parents had only dreamed of. If only he were here, even if only for one last drink on the veranda …

She sighed, finally pushing herself up from her chair. She ought to see about dinner, on the off chance Cullesil dragged the Earl back to Juelei. They'd need enough meat for an engagement feast, and a better wine than what they had in the cellars. She traipsed back into the house, the music once again drifting from the sitting room, playing an altogether different tune.

12

Two more days passed, the duke's ball quickly approaching, when a letter finally arrived. It wouldn't have been uncommon to pass the season in town with nothing to interrupt the endless days, but after the coup of the costume ball, it felt like uncovering a jewel. And it was only then she realized how desperately she had been waiting. Apparently, no matter how lovely the woods you hunted, if you were waiting for a large enough deer, the blind would eventually become intolerable.

She was breakfasting in the library with Cullesil — the woman hardly more than a ghost since she'd run off to get engaged — when Oeurelai came in with a letter on a silver tray. She cocked an eyebrow at it.

"Has this come in the post?" she asked, turning it over in her hands. The deep red envelope was addressed in a hand she didn't recognize.

"Private messenger, my lady," he said. "Didn't declare a house, though he came in a carriage."

She glanced at Cullesil, but the woman was lost in her own letter; a love missive no doubt. She broke the seal — bronze, in the shape of a lily — and unfolded the paper, which smelled mysteriously of honey blossoms. The letter within was only a single line.

Miss Shuwayel, if you should be without occupation, please do join myself and some acquaintances this afternoon in the Royal Gardens for high tea.

Lady Ceoretin Shailhun

She blinked, reading it three times before she dared believe it. The duke's sister, inviting *her* for tea? Her mind raced. The woman had done little more than glare at her at the ball, but this surely meant Lord Celanren, at least, was pleased with her. As Mother always said, if you got close to a powerful man, their family would always vet you. But if this was an invitation to audition for the role of duchess, what on

Wellonai would she wear?!

Without realizing it, she had shot out of her seat, the letter flung across the table. Cullesil took it up, her eyes widening by the word.

"But this is …" she said.

"I know!" Vorseyai exclaimed, dashing across the room to ring the bell for the maid. Ouerelai seemed surprisingly nonplussed — perhaps he really did want the butler job — simply stepping over to clear the breakfast things as Terin came in.

"My Lady?" she asked, curtseying.

"I need you to meet me in my rooms with Eserrion and every single dress in the house," she said, "and make it quick!"

The woman scurried back out into the hall, only making it halfway to the sitting room before she began calling for reinforcements.

"Well," Cullesil said, folding her napkin as she stood, "let's hop to it, eh? You'll want your hair done before you go about the dresses, I reckon."

Vorseyai nodded gratefully, and they moved into the corridor, walking quickly toward the stairs. Having her arm on Cullesil's seemed to provide some ballast, though it didn't seem to last long for either of them. Cullesil barely made it through three strokes of the hairbrush before their wide eyes met in the mirror.

"Great golden fields, Vorseyai, the *gardens* of all places!"

"I know," she said, breathlessly. Everyone who was anyone took more than a few turns in the gardens every season, but you didn't just stop there for tea … This was meant to awe her, of course, a reminder that Lady Shailhun was cousins with the empress. And perhaps they were rather awed at that, running about like bloody mulakerri … Still, that's precisely what training was for. No one liked to look out at a sea of enemies, but she wouldn't be caught with her sword in its sheath.

———

The rest of the morning soared by as they wasted most of their time arguing over dresses. Eserrion had fought valiantly for one of Mother's frumpier pieces, while she and Cullesil had a bitter argument over whether pink or chartreuse looked better with her skin tone. Eventually, they tore two dresses apart, the poor maid nearly working her fingers off to stitch them together.

Still, as she descended the stairs, she couldn't help but smile at herself in the mirror. They'd kept the skirt from Mother's dress, the dull rose color actually matching the light green bodice perfectly — like a flower in reverse. It was a bit springy for the summer heat, but it did wonders for her figure. For a moment, she almost thought Terin a man, her focus on accentuating her mistress's bosom most out of place for a maid who wore a frock all day …

Cullesil bade her farewell at the door, giving her a kiss on the cheek before she dashed across the gravel for the carriage house. She hadn't thought to ask for the carriage early, but when she pushed open the wide door, Jeotolm was already strapping the horses to the front, his livery on.

"Oh good," she said, moving toward the back, "I see Oeurelai told you to get ready?"

"Why, no, my lady," he said, making a quick bow as he offered her a hand up to the seat. "Mr. Seoyaln stopped in this morning on his way to Lord Heshan's, said you'd need a lift after lunch to the Sherolm Inn."

"Oh dear," Vorseyai said, her mind spinning. Seoyaln would be such a grouch if she didn't show, but the meeting with Lady Shailhun obviously had to take precedence. You could always grow more bloody plants, but an invitation like this may only come once in a lifetime!

"Unfortunately," she said, "I've had something important come up. I'll need you all afternoon, but perhaps you could run by the inn while I'm at tea and tell him not to expect me?"

"Of course, my lady," he said, bowing his head again.

The next moment, they were turning onto the road, heading toward the royal gardens. It only took two turns before it was visible on the horizon, like a city unto itself, the gardens surrounded by a giant wall of evergreen just under the palace terrace. Still, they had to criss-cross their way through the city to reach it, hurrying past the embassies to the top of the city.

After showing her invitation to a guard, they were shown through, driving under a giant arch in the pines. She'd never ridden a carriage into the gardens, though it seemed to do no harm to the wide paved rows between the plants. There was the usual army of workers, buzzing between the plants and the giant cistern in the center. The invitation hadn't said where they were to go, but one glance made it clear. Along the stairs to the palace, the widest terrace had a flag hanging from it bearing a bronze lily.

As they reached the stairs, she left the carriage behind, taking a parasol as she began the climb. She took the stairs only a few at a time, determined to avoid arriving out of breath and covered in sweat. Still, it was hard to deny the summer heat, and she felt damp beneath her arms as she reached the top.

She turned onto the tiny path that led to the terrace, finding two palace guards flanking an ivy-covered gate. The gardens were open to the public, of course, but it wasn't as though the empress's cousin couldn't demand some privacy on imperial property. She was about to reach for her invitation when the door wrenched open, an old man in livery looking out.

"Lady Vorseyai Shuwayel, I presume?" he asked, bowing slightly.

"Yes," she said, inclining her head.

"Splendid," he said, pulling the gate all the way open. "We saw your carriage arrive. If you'll follow me, the other ladies have just sat down to tea."

All of them? Her jaw clenched just a tiny bit more at being the last to arrive. She'd thought they would find her provincial if she arrived on time, though perhaps the others feared Lady Shailhun more than looking gauche …

She followed the butler down a winding path through the hedges before emerging onto the terrace, the sandstone platform baking in the sun. There, beneath a white umbrella, were three ladies, laughing as they took their tea. Lady Shailhun was facing her, wearing a pink dress and enough gems to open a bank. To her right was Lady Cheomkeln, and on her left, an older woman she didn't recognize.

"Lady Vorseyai Shuwayel," the butler said in a smooth voice. The other ladies didn't rise — which they technically didn't have to — but she curtseyed, approaching the open chair.

"Why, what an unusual dress," Lady Shailhun said, eyeing the material as if it were somehow poisonous. "It's as if the tailor made it in the dark."

Vorseyai blinked, forcing the smile to stay on her face. She did Mother's old trick to prevent her cheeks from flushing, pretending her face had been doused in ice.

"Yes, I dare say he did," she said, earning at least a chuckle from Lady Cheomkeln as she sat.

"It's certainly not something Taleomjen would ever make," Lady Shailhun said, still frowning. "Perhaps you've heard of my tailor, on Dilaom Street? He simply has the most marvelous eye. He picked out this silk for me."

"It looks lovely with your skin," the older lady said, nodding. She herself wore a silver dress that was decidedly unflattering, serving only to wash out her white hair. Still, she seemed about a hundred times friendlier than the others — even if that wasn't saying much.

"Vorseyai," Lady Shailhun said, "let me introduce you to Lady Meleong Miranil, Viscountess of Helayn and Tenth of Shadow House."

"A pleasure to meet you," Vorseyai said, smiling. So even a marquess and a viscountess followed Shailhun's lead ... That wasn't surprising, of course, but it was always important to know where the weight leaned at the tea table.

"Perhaps you know Lord Porsulair?" Vorseyai asked. "We're neighbors in the east, though I'm afraid I don't know how he fares in Shadow House."

Lady Miranil pursed her lips, looking off into the distance.

"I suppose it sounds somewhat familiar," she said, "though I can't say we're much in contact with relatives so far out. Shadow House lands are only a day's journey north, of course."

"Yes, where *is* Yuljeom?" Lady Cheomkeln asked, her attention on the tower of biscuits in the center of the table.

"My brother said it was the longest journey of his life," Lady Shailhun said, "though I must admit, I don't know myself either. Once you reach my station, there's hardly ever time to leave town. I don't even go to Fire House lands anymore if I can help it."

"Quite," Vorseyai said, taking a moment to pour herself some tea. If these women thought her an outlander, what would be the point of explaining where Yuljeom was, anyway? Which landmarks would they even know? "It's on the southern branch of the river, just north of the east bay."

Lady Cheomkeln nodded in interest, though Lady Shailhun had apparently already moved on.

"Oh, Meleong," she said to Lady Miranil, "you were going to tell me the name of that jeweler you used for Chulsedeom last year. I simply must have something new for my cousin's ball."

Another not so subtle show of power, referring to the empress as 'my cousin' and the royal holiday as 'a ball.' She had never been to the spring festival herself — it was much too hard to travel then — though perhaps if she played her cards right with the duke ...

"Oh, certainly," Lady Miranil replied. "I could take you tomorrow afternoon, if you're free. You'll simply adore her."

"Why, Vorseyai," Lady Shailhun said, turning to her with an innocent expression, "you probably have no idea what the spring ball is like, do you? Perhaps we could invite you next year, though I dare say the snow won't have melted off the country roads by then!"

The fire threatened her cheeks again, though this time, it was fueled by anger instead of shame. It's not that what Lady Shailhun said wasn't true — she'd just thought herself how hard spring travel was — but after the first comment, the insult in it was clear.

She almost opened her mouth with a sharp quip when Mother's voice entered her mind, a memory coming to her rescue at the last moment. It was from a time when she was preparing for her debut, before she could see the wisdom in any of the lessons. She had more or less asked Mother what the point of all their training was if she was already destined to be a baroness.

"Darling daughter," Mother had said, rolling her eyes, "this is Anushai. If they can depose the emperor with a single vote, you think they'll care if you're a baroness? They'd choose a pig over a queen if it knew the steps to dance."

It didn't matter who she was, or even whether Lord Celanren liked her or not. In fact, it wasn't about her at all. She may as well be that pig Mother warned her of. Of course, you had to be of rank to marry well, but Lady Shailhun probably already knew how much her estates earned within the penny. This was a test, pure and simple, and if she failed, Lady Nuyeln would still be waiting in the wings. But she had something no other woman had: she had Mother to guide her.

She smiled her most brilliant smile as she leaned in and squeezed Lady Shailhun's arm.

"So thoughtful of you," she said, her smile suddenly mirrored on Lady Shailhun's face, too contagious for spite to overcome. "It would be an honor, the snow notwithstanding." She finally broke her gaze, smiling at the other women. "I must say, everyone in town has been so kind, but especially Lord Celanren and his family. It's no wonder the empress hails from such a house."

"Hear, hear," Lady Cheomkeln said, murmuring in admiration. Lady Shailhun blinked in surprise, nodding before she took a hasty sip of her tea. Yes, a test indeed, but not one she was expected to pass.

"Well, you must be so excited for Lord Celanren's ball," Lady Miranil said to her, covering the silence. "You simply have to tell us what you're planning to wear. I dare say the duke will be wearing his red militia uniform."

That was it, her victory in a single phrase. The mere implication she might want to match the duke for his private ball was enough. Nothing could be clearer.

"Lady Shailhun did mention her tailor," Vorseyai said, inclining her head. "I don't suppose he could help me, but I'd love to have the proper colors for my first Fire House ball."

Lady Shailhun — finally seeming to recover from her surprise — put down her teacup, a thin smile coming to her face.

"I dare say, if you're free, we could go after tea," she said. "Mr. Taleomjen usually doesn't take clients without a proper introduction, though he'd happily fit you in for me."

"That would be wonderful," Vorseyai said, her smile genuine as she took a sip of her tea. It could have been the honey in her cup, but suddenly, the world seemed delightfully sweet.

13

Three hours later, Vorseyai rushed back up the stairs of Juelei Hall, Jeotolm close behind her with a giant dress box in hand. They had gone to see the acclaimed Mr. Taleomjen, and he had been everything Lady Shailhun was not. After a brief introduction, he seemed to think her a goddess, worthy of every adoration as he wrapped her in the most sumptuous fabric the empire had to offer.

In the end, of course, she'd been forced to spend nearly a month's income on the thing, though that was likely just another part of the test. Still, it would be worth every penny when she arrived at Lord Celanren's ball. When Lady Shailhun herself had seen it, a sort of strange, ironic smile came to her lips. She seemed to know exactly what it would mean for her brother when Vorseyai climbed the stairs to his ball, her figure perfected by the folds of scarlet silk.

She rushed past the valet who opened the door for her, pointing Jeotolm up the stairs as she prepared to look for Cullesil, an afternoon's worth of gossip ready to burst from her lips.

"Where were you?" a deep voice asked from the sitting room. She turned, finding Mr. Seoyaln in the parlor, his coat off and his sleeves rolled up as if he'd just come in from outside. He was leaning with his elbows on his knees, looking up at her from under his brow. It was a presumptuous way to address her, being little more than a gardener, but for some reason those forearms struck her, the thick hair and tight muscles jumping out in her mind. If she could ignore the thundercloud on his face, she'd almost think him handsome.

She took a deep breath, raising herself up.

"I do feel badly I couldn't give you notice, Mr. Seoyaln, but I had something important to take care of in the city. I trust you had the meeting well in hand without me?"

"I should say not," he said, sighing as he stood, turning to face the front windows. Without realizing it, she stepped toward him. "Lady

Cruseln was very offended you didn't show. She decided not to buy the medicine after all."

"Well, I should think my presence wouldn't matter if she were really serious. What did Lord Heshan make of it?"

"Or maybe she wanted to see if *you* were really serious," he said, anger flashing in his eyes as he looked at her. "What is she to do if she picks our supply over another and you abandon the crop in a season? What of her patients? I'm not presumptuous enough to think my position in your house is guaranteed, and if you're too busy playing at tea to see to things, what then? People could die, Vorseyai."

She set her jaw, biting back the curse she wanted to fling at him. This was really too much! He used her name like a commoner and still had the audacity to tell her she was *playing*? After what she'd just accomplished for this house? The house he bloody relied on to pay for his damned plants, by the way! When she finally felt in control enough to speak, she nearly scared herself with the ice in her voice.

"*Playing*, Mr. Seoyaln? I'd have you remember I am the lady of this house — a baroness, mind you — and this playing at tea is the only business my life may ever amount to. I dare say, if I'm successful at the *one* thing my life was designed for, I could buy every hospital in the kingdom. You may care for them, but it is my estate that supports those plants. In fact, if it weren't for my mother's coin, Father's playthings would have withered long before you arrived. Remember your place. You are a guest in my house, the tenure of which is — as you so aptly put — decidedly *not* guaranteed."

They stood, staring at each other for a long moment, the silence pregnant with rage and offense. But then, something in him shifted, and he looked toward the floor.

"You're right," he said quietly, his mouth forming a thin line. "I apologize if I've overstepped. It's only, your father always spoke of you as if … Well, never mind." His voice lowered to a whisper, as if talking to himself. "I suppose for all my time in the greenhouse I really haven't learned anything after all."

Mr. Seoyaln took a deep breath, meeting her eyes. He looked at her for a long moment, his mouth half-open. For an instant, it seemed as if he'd beg her to forgive him. In fact, it looked as if he'd bloody propose, if they were lovers. But then, he let out a breath, time resuming its endless march as he shook his head.

"I won't do you the dishonor of staying on once I've besmirched you," he said. "I shall return to Borimol at once and pack my things. There will be a few things to sort out with the plants, but I should be gone by the time you return." He met her eyes again, smiling sadly. "Please do take care of yourself, Lady Shuwayel. It's been an honor to be in your service."

He nodded, turning to go. She blinked, her mouth hanging open as he disappeared around the corner. Part of her wanted to call him back — to undo what she'd said, to ask what he'd meant bringing up Father, to buy herself a bloody moment to think — but she swallowed the words in her throat.

Where she was going, there wouldn't be any room for the boundless frivolity of the greenhouse. She'd do far more good on the path she'd chosen with the duke. In the end, it was Mother who had won the day again. Father's dreams would have to go, and they would have to take Mr. Seoyaln with them.

———

Once Seoyaln left, Vorseyai wandered through the house in a daze, her head still swimming with arguments she wished she'd made. But why did it matter, if he admitted she was right? He was gone and that was the end of it. Eventually she found Cullesil in her bedroom, reading in a nook by the fireplace. Cullesil wasn't normally much for reading, but she didn't seem to have the energy to question it. Besides, the long summers could do strange things to people. She barely managed to turn herself as she reached the bed, flopping down in a puff of silk and sighing as she stared at the ceiling.

"Was tea … bad, then?" Cullesil asked, marking her page as she put the book down.

"No," Vorseyai said, "it was … incredible."

It *was* incredible, and she ought to be celebrating it, not staring at the little cherubs on the ceiling and wishing she could join them.

"Well, that's good," Cullesil said, sitting gently beside her on the bed. She took Vorseyai's hand, patting it. "After the last ball, I was honestly a little worried they'd be mean to you."

"Oh, no, they were awful," Vorseyai said, chuckling. She pulled herself up, leaning on her elbow. "They did everything they could to insult me — my dress, our county — but I didn't rise to the bait, and that was all I needed to do, apparently. Lady Shailhun took me dress shopping afterward and everything. I daresay she approves now."

A flash of anger showed on Cullesil's face. Borimol may have been the county seat, but it was Cullesil's farms that made Yuljeom the pride of the coast.

"At any rate," Vorseyai continued, flopping back down on the bed, "I suppose we should all wish to be so rich that we can be as horrid as those women."

"Maybe …" Cullesil said, turning thoughtful. "Though, Lord Porsulair — er, I suppose I ought to call him Hoylan, now — says those of rank owe it to the kingdom to be the best of us. Otherwise, what's the point, right?"

"Hmm," Vorseyai hummed. "I agree in principle, certainly, though I'm not sure Lady Shailhun would subscribe to your philosophy."

"I suppose not," Cullesil said. "We'll just have to hope you can be a good influence on them."

"I think I'll have my chance at that," Vorseyai said, smiling in spite of herself. "Say, what were you reading anyway? I dare say that's not your … um … usual amusement."

Cullesil hit her on the arm, but sprang up from the bed, returning with the small green book.

"Lord— Hoylan asked me to read it," she said, showing her the cover. *Neleom Kelshun*, it read, a donkey etched on the front. "I suppose he really does want to make a go of the farms with me, silly man. He has the fortune to avoid any labor if he wanted. Anyway, he wants me reading up on the latest science, see if we can't whip the old plots by the river into shape — you know, the low-yielding ones Father refuses to work."

"That's wonderful," Vorseyai said, smiling even though she suddenly felt very sad. It seemed impossible to imagine living without Cullesil by her side, but if she were to become a duchess, she'd likely be just as tied to the city as Lady Shailhun. She sat up, pulling her friend into a tight embrace.

"What's all this?" Cullesil asked, patting the back of her head.

"I just … thank you," she said, sniffing as she held in a tear. "I couldn't have done all this without you."

"Nor I you," Cullesil said, laughing. "And we'll do the rest together. I can't wait to be at your wedding."

They both finally began laughing again as they gushed about what their weddings would be like. The sun lit the room in gold as it set, the gauzy light shining like the future itself. For a moment, things didn't seem to hurt so badly, and the weight of the world drifted away in a moment of brightness, a moment too precious to let go.

14

When the day finally arrived, the duke's ball proved to be everything Lord Cheomkeln's was not. There were no costumes, no secret introductions through the butler, only the resplendent glory of society at its height. It would be a lie to say she didn't feel a thrill as she walked in, her new dress swishing over the marble steps of a place she dreamed of calling her own. Cheorin Hall may have been one of the youngest mansions in the city, but it was easily the most beautiful, too, its windows shining against the night as the city revolved around it.

It was only when they entered the ballroom that Vorseyai truly stopped dreaming, coming back to her senses as Cullesil squeezed her hand. She looked up, finding Lord Celanren at the head table in the finest military dress she had ever seen, his gold buttons shining brighter than the chandelier. He was speaking to his sister, but his gaze suddenly turned to her, a sort of … satisfaction appearing on his face. She didn't want to delude herself, but perhaps there was a hint of ownership in that gaze, an ownership she would gladly submit to if she could be queen of this place.

She smiled before turning away, waving to Lady Miranil as she broke off from the Cullesil and Lord Porsulair. Unfortunately, their seat assignments were far apart — her star not so ascendent as to make Cullesil's rank irrelevant — but her star *was* ascending … Every eye seemed to follow her as she crossed the room, with more than a few women hiding behind their fans to gossip as she passed. Tea with the duke's sister was hardly anything to gossip over, of course, though there was a notable lack of swan-shaped actresses in the room …

"Why, Vorseyai," Lady Miranil said, taking her hand as she reached the table, "your dress is just as lovely as Lady Shailhun promised."

Of course, the viscountess would use her given name — at least until she was a bloody duchess! — but she still smiled.

"It really is," Vorseyai said, holding up the fabric and twirling for the older woman. "It's like wearing a cloud!"

They passed the next few minutes with idle banter, Lord Miranil joining them to introduce himself as the band began to tune their instruments. She met a few more lords and ladies whose names she would struggle mightily to retain, and then, she looked up, spotting Cullesil chatting with Lord Heshan across the room. She made her excuses to Lady Miranil, moving quickly toward the pair.

"Lord Heshan," she said, curtseying, "I am so very sorry I had to miss the meeting with Lady Cruseln. I do hope it didn't prove too inconvenient for you."

"Not at all," he said, smiling. "I do know what it's like to be a certain age about town. In fact, I was just congratulating Cullesil on her engagement."

"Yes," Vorseyai said, squeezing Cullesil's hand, "I am so very pleased for them."

"Perhaps, though …" Lord Heshan said, lowering his voice, "I could have a word?"

She inclined her head, and they took a step away from the others.

"I don't wish to spoil such a gay night, of course," he said, finally frowning, "but Lord Seoyaln did stay with me one night while he left for Borimol."

"Ah," Vorseyai said, taking a deep breath. "I am truly—"

"No, no," Lord Heshan said, raising a hand, "you've nothing to apologize for. The lad told me he spoke more harshly than he'd have liked, but he did leave a letter for you." He dug into his pocket, holding up a small envelope. "I only hope you'll forgive him. I think he's too ashamed to ask to keep his post, but I hope you'll consider for my sake. Lord Seoyaln is so very dedicated to you and your father."

She frowned, taking the letter. What was all this 'Lord Seoyaln' business? Surely Lord Heshan of all people could use the man's given name, especially if he was a friend of the boy's own father! Still, what was she to do?

"I … believe I may have been overly harsh myself," she said. "I promise to write to him — I'd hate to have fences unmended — but it's his decision if he stays or goes. He's left to pack his things, and I'm not sure any letter I write could reach him in time."

"That's all I ask," Lord Heshan said, smiling as he squeezed her shoulder. "You are such a lovely person, Lady Shuwayel. Thank you, truly."

With that, he bowed, making his way toward the wine. She stood there for a moment, her mouth still half-open with something she'd wanted to say, a lump in her throat that was … what, regret? At this, her most important hour? She meant what she said, she *did* want to mend things with Seoyaln, but she certainly didn't regret what she'd done either! How could she, when this was the result? She'd be lying if she said she wasn't still rehashing arguments with the man in her head, but there was no room for that tonight!

She allowed herself one quiet growl before she forced a smile back onto her face, turning to find someone else to talk to. But just then, the dinner bell rang, forcing her to spin about again, trying not to stomp her feet as she marched back to her table.

The dinner was a maddening mix of pleasure and pain, the night still magical but unable to completely banish the drudgery of a seated dinner. With Lady Miranil at her table, she had to stay on her guard as well, making the most boring conversation imaginable as she picked through a pound of food. But holy god of gold, was that food incredible! The duke had brought in game from his lands in the north, the pheasant so soft she'd thought for a moment it was molded from butter — not to mention the wines, desserts, and thousand other delicacies passing her seat.

If she were able to land the duke, she'd have to be extremely careful with her figure. A feast like this at Borimol would have seen her rolled away from the table at the end. Luckily, Mother's '6-1-2' rule was there to guide her through the meal, the conversation meandering through six speakers before she took a bite, with two sips of wine between cycles. It kept her from looking like a woman watching her figure without tossing said figure into the flames with reckless abandon.

Finally, the dinner music came to an end, the band marching toward the dance floor. A ripple of excitement passed through the room, the guests beginning to stand as the servants clearing dishes suddenly vanished. Vorseyai made some kind of excuse as she left her table, floating toward the dance floor with the others as she watched the duke from the corner of her eye.

Despite everything she'd been through so far, *this* was the deciding moment, the test that would prove the crucible of every other effort she'd made. The dancing tonight was to be open — no bloody *essom'tiluw* or *eldenshin* — simply the men choosing the women, their flaws and virtues laid bare like a hunk of meat at the butchers.

She ended up on the far side of the dance floor, clutching Cullesil's arm with a fresh glass of wine inexplicably in her hand. She sipped it — racking her brain for when she'd picked up the cursed thing — while she ran through all of Mother's exercises for cooling the flush from her skin.

Finally, though, the band was tuned, and the room filled with a pregnant silence, every eye turning toward the duke. There was a moment that seemed to last forever as he looked over his guests, his usual wicked smile on his face. Then … the impossible happened. He locked eyes with her, his smile deepening by a hair as he stepped toward her.

"My Lady," he said, giving her the merest glimmer of a bow, "would you do me the honor of the first dance?"

She couldn't even speak, simply nodding as a quick tap from Cullesil reminded her to curtsey. The duke offered her his arm, and she took it, bobbing like a ship in a storm as he led her to the center of the dance floor. The musicians began to play the moment they were in place, a few bars of whirling violin serving as a warning for the waltz to come as the rest of the party began pairing off. The duke took her waist, his eyes on hers for one last moment as they began to dance.

"That is a lovely dress," he said over the music, his face still calm, as if a lifetime on stage made keeping the beat of no particular consequence.

"Thank you," she said, forcing herself to smile without missing her steps. "Your sister introduced me to her tailor."

"Ah," the duke said, nodding as if he didn't already know. "Taleomjen's a good chap — early customer of my father's."

She nodded. So at least the outrageous price was for a good cause …

"You must miss him dearly," she said.

"The tailor?" he asked, meeting her eyes again as he raised an eyebrow.

"No, your father," she said, chuckling.

"Oh," he said, "yes, I suppose I must. Perhaps I could take you to see his theatre, show you the family history and all that."

"That would be lovely," she said, smiling again.

He nodded, putting all his energy back into the dancing, but he squeezed her hip a little tighter, at least signaling she hadn't overstepped.

She continued to spin with him, tempted to close her eyes as she tried to savor the moment for all it was worth. Still, eventually the song had to end, and they ended up back in the center of the dance floor, the duke finally letting go of her, her limbs suddenly limp after all his strength had held them up.

"My Lord," she said curtseying as she stepped back.

The entire room was suddenly watching them again, a hundred eyes on the folds of her red dress. Thankfully, Cullesil appeared from the crowd, taking her elbow and guiding her back to the edge while the duke moved toward his next partner — this one, a delightfully ancient woman.

She suddenly had decidedly more suitors than before, but every other dance hardly mattered after the first, her attention on the duke regardless of which man had her arm. He seemed to keep an eye on her, too, their eyes meeting every now and again as he gave her that predatory glare. He almost seemed as if he might duel her other partners for daring to touch her. She smiled each time before twirling away, somehow hoping he might do just that.

When the gong was finally rung for the final dance, he returned, asking her for one last turn. They didn't speak that time, simply moving to the music, though his eyes never left hers. She stared back at him, simply trying to catch her breath as the world felt like it might go on spinning forever. As the song finally ended and the guests began to clap, the duke looked her over, his lips pursed as if appraising a bolt of cloth.

"Perhaps …" he said slowly, "you'd join me on the veranda?"

———

Like the rest of the house, "veranda" proved to be the wrong word entirely. The massive stone structure looked more like a stage as it curved from the ballroom toward the sea. There were a few couples out there already — mostly ones that hadn't seemed keen on the dancing, though from the way the women giggled in the darkness, it seemed they'd found something more amusing.

"I daresay we made a decent show of it tonight," the duke said.

She turned back from the water to find his eyes on her, the view apparently already perfectly ordinary to him.

"They do say dancing is all in the partner," she replied, grinning. "The dress did all the work on my end, but I may have to get a whole wardrobe in red after seeing the results."

"I think we can arrange that," he said, suddenly serious. He cleared his throat, stepping closer. "I suppose I wasn't entirely sure until tonight," he said, "but … father always said only a fool lets someone else buy the wool once they've had it weighed."

She felt her mouth go dry. She'd started to hope, of course, but hadn't dared dream the moment could come so soon …

"I wondered," he continued, "if you might like to marry me."

He pulled a golden bracelet from his pocket, opening it with a click. It wasn't the most romantic proposal she'd ever heard, but he actually bowed at the waist, holding the bracelet before her. It was a beautiful piece, with giant stripes of ruby swirling through the gold.

"Y-yes," she stammered before the proper words came to her. "May

Essomuai shine through this circle, lighting it for all of my days."

She gently put her wrist inside, and he looked up at her, clicking it shut as he took her hands. He genuinely smiled for a moment before he looked back to the ballroom.

"I suppose I ought to have some wine brought up for a toast. It's best to announce these things when you're hosting, saves you embarrassing someone else at their ball."

"Right," she said, nodding slowly. "I suppose you're right."

He nodded, turning to ring the bell for his butler.

"Perhaps, though," she added quickly, "we might take just a moment for a more … private celebration?"

"Ah, yes," he said, nodding, "how silly of me."

He gripped her by the waist, his hands powerful as he dipped her, kissing her on the mouth. It was nothing like any kiss she'd had before — even if those had been furtive, boyish things. It was raw and animalistic, the kiss of someone who never once waited for what they wanted. She closed her eyes, melting into it as her head spun with his cologne. There would be time enough to teach him gentleness, of course. But for now, she would embrace his passion for the inferno it was. This man was to be her husband, and he was simply claiming what was his.

He released her, pulling her back up as he smoothed his jacket, his eyes suddenly glassy in the lamplight.

"Well," she said, catching her breath, "that is precisely what I had in mind."

He chuckled, offering her his arm as he led her back into the ball, a lifetime of promise waiting within.

15

The next afternoon, Vorseyai finally found time to sit down at her desk, her head spinning from all the excitement. They hadn't even set a date, but Juelei had been a maelstrom all morning, the list of preparations nearly a mile long already. Luckily, Eserrion had filled in for Mother as her head general, barking at the maids as they dashed about, preparing the house to entertain while Oeurelai frantically wrote up lists of things to be sent for at Borimol.

Thankfully though, despite the chaos, she'd found time to visit her parents' crypt before lunch, desperate to tell them the news in person before the wedding became all-consuming. Frankly, it was lucky she went when she did. Father's grave was in desperate need of attention after how long she had been stuck in mourning. She cried as she swept the stone, though they'd been tears of joy, her voice cracking as she told him the news — and everything other thing she'd kept inside for the last year.

Now she only had about an hour until the duke came for her — a card delivered that morning offering her the promised theatre tour. But there was one last thing she had to do before she could ride off to victory. She had promised Lord Heshan she would write to Mr. Seoyaln, and she intended to keep her promise. If this was to be her first day as the future Lady Celanren, she would leave her life as Lady Shuwayel done right.

She broke the seal, finding a surprisingly long letter inside. She'd seen his writing before, of course, on little notes and things at the house, but now his hand seemed surprisingly elegant for a gardener.

Dearest Vorseyai,

I truly hope this letter finds you well. I'll be leaving for Borimol tomorrow to pack my things, but I couldn't bear to go without setting things right. I'm so very sorry for the way I spoke to you. I overstepped, and in so doing, I'm afraid I was also horribly unfair. I would never want to speak harshly of one such as you, a woman who has more goodness than any I've had the pleasure to meet.

I know I've put too much pressure on you over the years, but I promise it's only because I regard you so highly. Still, even without the greenhouse you truly are already the best woman I've known. This may come as a surprise for something that comes so naturally to you, but I think it no secret that the staff at Borimol adore you. You have always treated everyone in the county with kindness and care, things that are all too rare in a lady of your station. Even when I was little more than a bother to you, you always made me feel welcome at Borimol, a place I will always consider a home.

However, I also hope you don't think I'm writing to secure my employment. The greenhouse has been a dream, but I think it's time we all woke up. I have learned invaluable lessons from you and your father, lessons I will carry with me all of my days. May Essomuai bless you, and may you have every success and joy you seek in life.

Yours sincerely,
  Keristal Seoyaln

She blinked in surprise, letting the letter drop onto the desk as she stared into space. How oddly … heartfelt. She'd actually likely never received a letter so full of kindness, not even from the few suitors who had swirled about after her debut. He was right to apologize, of course, but it was obvious now he could only speak the way he had because he cared for her and her family so. She took a deep breath, closing her eyes. She had already planned what she wanted to write him in return, but now she felt sure it was right. She couldn't change what she had to do, but he deserved the same kindness in return.

She took a piece of stationery from the desk, smoothing it before her as she set out her writing things. She started with her seal, carefully melting the wax over the candle. The ritual suddenly felt sacred, as each time she used it now would be approaching her last. What did the Celanren seal look like? It felt absurd to imagine using scarlet wax after thousands of letters sealed in green, but it would also be a delight when it matched the rubies on her wrist.

She carefully addressed the envelope, the heavy bracelet dragging across the paper — however did women get used to that? Her arm felt like a stranger's, her words taking on a strange tilt as she pulled her pen across the page. It actually took two wasted envelopes to get it right, but finally she seemed to get the hang of it, moving down to the parchment as she started her letter, letting the words form before she second guessed herself.

Dear Mr. Seoyaln,

I thank you for your letter, and I hope you will forgive me for any harshness on my part when last we spoke. I do accept your apology, though I think in many ways, you only spoke the truth, honoring my father's legacy as you were hired to do.

She paused, absently running the back of her quill along her face. She pictured herself back at the tombs, the ratty old broom in her hand as she swept the entrance to Father's crypt. With all that debris piled up, there had seemed a great irony in mourning. Sitting in black for a year at Borimol was meant to honor the people she most loved in the world, while the only monument left to them gathered dust on the mountain.

I'm afraid that in my attempts to honor Father, I rather lost sight of the purpose behind the greenhouse. Those herbs are meant to help people, and you were justified in your rebuke of me. If I kept them from a hospital, I would no more honor Father than I would if I were to fire all the staff at Borimol.

She closed her eyes, taking a deep breath. It was the truth, as hard as it was to say, though she still at least had the distance of a letter to protect her. Would he understand this apology? Or would he only think her more foolish than he already did? In the end, it probably mattered little. She was to be a duchess in Fire House now, and the fate of the greenhouse was already sealed. The question was, what would become of their contents.

In addition to writing to you today, I am also sending a letter of apology to Lady Cruseln. I hope she will overlook my slight in favor of her patients. That is the second reason for my letter. As you said, the greenhouse has been a dream in many ways, but I believe it's time it closed. I am to be married, and it's time I shift my focus to town. Still, I want each and every herb in the place to help someone. If you would stay on to help me in that, it would be a great honor to both Father and myself.

Your friend,
   Lady Vorseyai Shuwayel

She finally let out her breath, slumping back in her chair as she reached for the bell. If Oeurelai could send this letter along with everything else headed for Borimol, it would reach him by the end of the week. Assuming he didn't toss it in the fire and storm off the estates, there was still time to bring Father's work to fruition. And yet ... why did her heart seem to ache so? Had she really grown sentimental for a forest of weeds?

She closed her eyes, picturing the greenhouse, her walk in the gardens every day. Perhaps it was losing that time in her life — lonely as it had been — when it had been just her and Borimol. And maybe, if she was being truly honest with herself, she really would miss the friend she'd made in Mr. Seoyaln, waiting for her every day with his little book. They had built something together in the short time they'd had, and even when he drove her mad, his letter proved he *was* a friend, if nothing else.

She shook her head, carefully sealing the letter before she stood. It *was* a good letter, but sentiment was no reason for frivolity. She simply couldn't keep the greenhouse. The duke was first and foremost a businessman, and while her fortune would add substantially to his, he would never let her spend that money on proper care for their staff if she frittered away its twentieth each year on a bunch of plants.

"My lady?" Oeurelai asked, bowing as he entered the room. He seemed on tenterhooks since she announced her engagement that morning, as if he thought she might cast him on the street. Surely the duke would keep his butler, but the man looked to be nearly eighty, and she would never allow one of her own footmen to be cast aside.

"Send this letter to Borimol," she said, handing it to him. "And send for Terin. Lord Celanren will be here soon, and I must be dressed for a carriage ride."

"Right away, my lady," he said, bowing again as he backed from the room. Yes, things were changing, and quickly. But the battle would be worth the blood when victory arrived. She had to believe that.

16

As Vorseyai rode through town in the duke's carriage, it felt very much like being on stage — which, of course, was likely the intended effect. It was an open-topped monstrosity, gleaming white and covered in golden scrollwork. It was not her style, certainly, but it was as good a time as any to begin adapting, marrying into Fire House as she was. More importantly, the day was perfect. There was a breeze coming in from the ocean, and enough clouds that her hat — which she'd forced Terin to trim with red feathers — could act as more than a sunshade.

The duke sat with his back to the driver, pointing out everything around town as if she'd never seen it before. Still, it was telling to see things through his eyes — especially the raised eyebrows indicating what he thought she should be wowed by. Still, when they finally reached the theatre, it was hard to keep her eyes from widening. She had heard of the Delhul, of course, though she hadn't attended a play there — or many plays of any kind, for that matter.

If you were to be the queen of any realm, though, this was an enviable domain, the structure nearly as large as the palace itself. It was arranged like a seat for some giant god, with two large wings on the side and a soaring loft on the back. Lady Eltinear — the only person she knew personally who'd attended a play there — had said the set pieces seemed to fly in from nowhere, a maze of ropes and pulleys dropping them from the sky.

"Marvelous, isn't it?" Lord Celanren asked, wearing the most genuine smile she'd ever seen on him.

"Yes, completely," she said, nodding as she turned back to him.

"Well, come on," he said, gesturing for the driver to help them down. "There isn't anything on today, and you ought to see the stage."

If there was anything to make one feel like a duchess in training, it was walking into the Delhul in the middle of the day. Not a single door was closed to them as they approached, liveried staff bowing as they

95

swept through the gilded lobby and into the auditorium. They stopped at the top of the stairs, the rows of fine seats descending below as sweeping balconies lifted up to either side. The curtain was closed, though the blood-red silk almost glistened in the lamplight.

"That's the curtain that started it all," the duke said reverently, his hands on his hips as he stared down at the stage.

"It *is* very fine," Vorseyai said, tapping her lips with her gloved hand. "But how did he turn it into such a prosperous business?"

"Foresight, I suppose," he said, "and … hunger."

She raised an eyebrow at that, but the duke's eyes never left the stage.

"My father simply had to have the best. When he couldn't find anyone to supply the quality he wanted, he sourced his own silk. Then he hired his own seamstresses. By the time customers were interested, he already had a team ready to take on nearly every new order for fabrics in the kingdom."

"Foresight, indeed," she agreed, her eyes wandering up to the frescos painted on the ceiling.

"I should say so," the duke said, finally turning toward her. "The factory makes twenty times in a year what the theatre does."

She blinked at that. It was hardly a review of family finances — not when she had no clue how much a theatre earned — but it did rather seem an admission of how their lives were about to be intertwined.

"If only," he added, taking a deep breath, "I could see as clearly as he saw." He shook his head. "Father seemed to trip over money, but what comes after textiles? I suppose that's why we'll make a good match; everyone in Fire House seems to think the same."

"Why, Lord Celanren," she said, tapping him on the arm, "that's very nearly an admission of fallibility on your part. I dare say you are one of a kind."

"Yes, quite," he said, frowning, not seeming to see the joke.

"Well," she said, clearing her throat, "I'd be very pleased to assist in any way I can, of course."

"Right," he said, his frown deepening by a shade.

So it wasn't her he was expecting to contribute? Her fortune was certainly reasonable enough, but it wasn't as though she had any Grass House relatives who were geniuses at business … Suddenly, her mouth seemed quite dry. It was all well and good when their interactions were limited to dancing and eyelash-batting, but she'd lose the bloody engagement if she couldn't learn to hold a conversation with the man! She wetted her lips, about to offer at least some other comment when the doors to the theatre opened again, the sound of arguing spilling in with the afternoon light.

She turned around, finding Lady Nuyeln storming past the doormen, a red-faced lady's maid scurrying at her heels. Luckily, the duke was already frowning, but as Lady Nuyeln stopped before him to curtsey, he raised a hand, her liveried pursuers bowing before disappearing back into the hall.

"Lord Celanren," Lady Nuyeln said, smiling. "I was hoping I'd catch you here before the show."

Catch him, indeed … It'd be impossible to miss his carriage, of course, and her hair looked a shade too perfect for a chance encounter.

"Lady Nuyeln," he said, nodding, "it appears you're in luck. In future, however, please do use the service entrance."

"Why, of course," she said, "I only wanted to make sure I saw you personally. We do need to discuss the issue of the set piece in the third act again."

"Very well," he said. "I'm engaged at the moment, but I promise to stop by before the show and discuss it with Lukeirn." He raised a hand, gesturing to Vorseyai.

"I believe you know my fiancée?" he asked.

Lady Nuyeln looked in her direction for the first time, a momentary frown escaping through her smile. Even if her invitation to the duke's ball evaporating had been a strong hint, she looked as if she really hadn't heard.

"Ah, yes," she said. "Remind me what your name was again?"

"Lady Vorseyai Shuwayel," she answered with her most winning smile. "Though don't feel bad for forgetting. I suppose I'll be a Celanren before long."

The woman's eyes bulged like a bug's before she could stop them with a blink, the smile forcibly returning to her face.

"Yes, quite," she said, turning back to the duke. "Well, I ought to get to the dressing room. Please do, er … stop by later."

"Certainly," the duke said, nodding again as he stepped aside, gesturing for her to pass.

"What a bother," he said to himself before looking up, seeming to have forgotten Vorseyai for a moment. "How about we finish our tour? We should have time for tea afterward if we make good time to the factory."

"I'm completely in your hands," Vorseyai said, inclining her head before following him back to the street.

———

Back in the carriage, they moved quickly through the city, heading south toward the sea before they turned along the coast. Before long, they were passing the temple stream into the southwest quarter, the palatial homes giving way to warehouses and tenements. The streets were visibly more crowded, and there were pockets of Alaran refugees milling about, their odd clothes visible even at a distance.

"Poor souls," Vorseyai said, her eyes lingering on one man on a corner wrapped in a blanket, his coughs so loud she could hear them across the street.

"Hmm?" the duke asked, looking up from some papers he was trying to sort before they reached the factory. He followed her eyes before returning to his business. "Yes, they are rather pitiful."

"I suppose we really will do some good with the greenhouse, at least," Vorseyai said. "Sickness must move awfully fast through these crowds."

"You're still interested in that nonsense?" he asked without looking up.

"No, well, I—"

She paused, clenching her teeth. She was about to tell him about wrapping up the greenhouse, but there was something quite off about his tone. Surely she wouldn't have time for it once they married, but it *was* Father's legacy, and a timely one by the look of things.

She took a deep breath, calming herself. The duke was a bit mercenary, of course, but that wasn't anything she didn't know. And she'd certainly heard the way they spoke of the war at Lord Cheomkeln's ball. She simply had to trust she'd be a moderating influence on him once her position was secure.

"I plan to wrap it up," she continued, "though I still want to distribute what we've already grown. I daresay it could do some good here. I suppose I hadn't realized how bad it was on this side of town."

"Well, I say never throw a thing away if it can fetch some coin," he said.

He looked up, narrowing his eyes as he watched the street, as if measuring how much coin he could get for her herbs if a plague swept through the tenements.

"Anyway," he said, shaking his head, "we're very nearly there. I apologize for the roughness of the area, but the factory is really something."

Finally, the carriage slowed, reaching a neighborhood along the water filled with giant brick warehouses. As they turned off the high street, a pair of beggars on the corner caught sight of their carriage.

"Please, sir!" one of them cried out, gesturing with his cap in hand, "a coin for the poor!"

Pedestrians were darting to and fro on the street, and the carriage had to slow to take the turn. The other beggar, this one with a crutch under his arm, started hobbling toward the carriage. He moved quickly despite what appeared to be an amputation, and in a moment he was abreast of them.

"Please, sir," he said, huffing with the effort of keeping up, "just one coin, sir."

Vorseyai reached for her bag. Father had always given full sovereigns to anyone they passed in the city who needed help, and she ought to continue the tradition once she was a duchess, surely. She had her hand on her coin purse when a flash passed in front of her eyes, a whip connecting with the beggar's face with a sickening crack. She looked up in horror to find Lord Celanren with the weapon in hand, whipping at the man twice more as he fell back.

"I said to take the corners quickly, Joersem!" the duke yelled at the driver as he threw the whip back to him, his face a cloud of darkness.

"Yes m'lord," the driver said, nodding with a stony face.

"Scum," the duke muttered under his breath as he turned toward the closest building, pointing at a painted sign that read Celanren Clothworks.

"Here we are," he said, smoothing his jacket. "And not a moment too soon."

Vorseyai looked back at the beggar as the coach pulled away, the duke's words drifting past her without registering. Her purse was still in her hand, on the brink of removing some coins. Her lips parted involuntarily, her eyes blinking slowly as she tried to absorb the thoughts bubbling up. But of everything swimming through her mind, there was only one thing she could cling to: *Seoyaln was right.*

Everything she'd done, everything she'd planned was … meaningless. She had thought herself so clever, so far above the whirling of the pool. In the end, though, she was a fool, no different from the rest. Father had at least tried to help people. Even if his plants took a hundred years to cultivate, at least he had tried. But what had she done, exactly? Traded her womb for a gilded life in town? Ten thousand crowns could go a long way, but it was an awfully high price for your soul.

She shook her head, squeezing her eyes shut as she sucked in a breath.

"Lord Celanren," she said, "I need to go home."

He turned toward her, his brow furrowed in confusion. The beggar may as well have been a bit of rubbish under his carriage wheel.

"Home?" he asked. "But we've only just arrived. Surely you'll want to see the factory first."

She squared her shoulders, giving him a faint smile, far more than he deserved.

"No I think I'd better not," she said, her voice firm. "You see, I just realized there's somewhere I need to be, and I've already delayed far too long."

She chuckled, shaking her head as she reached for the bracelet on her wrist, unclasping it as she tossed it to him.

"Joersem," she called to the driver, "if you'd stop for me, please."

The carriage came to a halt, and she stood, still smiling at the duke, whose face had turned the color of a building fire.

"My lord duke," she said, "I daresay I hope to never see you again."

She dropped down onto the cobblestones without waiting for the driver's help, a coin already in hand to help the man the duke had whipped.

Suddenly, everything felt so clear, so obvious it made her want to laugh. She didn't love the duke: she loved Mr. Seoyaln. It seemed almost too preposterous to say out loud, but the moment she'd thought of him, he'd come rushing into her mind, every muscle and hair already burned into her memory. For all his bloody piety, he was a *good* man, a man like Father, whose title didn't determine the way he walked through the world. He was a man who knew her, the her she'd actually been raised to be, before the balls and dresses had blinded her to what was right. And if she were being honest with herself, as she'd read his letter, she'd thought — no, hoped — he loved her too.

As she crossed the street, the beggar was still there, and she waved to him, hurrying over. He had a dark welt forming on his face, but he looked all right, nothing a trip to her family doctor couldn't fix. But for once, she could help someone — really help them — and when that was done, she'd find a carriage home before it was too late to tell the truth.

17

A week later, Vorseyai finally reached Borimol, the house lifting up before her in the afternoon sun, at once both terribly familiar and like some relic of a time long past. Her fingernails were nubs and her hair had the look of a bird's nest, but none of that could prevent her leaping from the carriage the moment it stopped. Not even Merishail could stop her, the man blanching as she stormed through the house.

"My lady!" he cried, turning to follow her. "We didn't expect you!"

And nor should he! She'd forced Jeotolm to drive through the night, for once forsaking every step of Mother's itinerary through the countryside, in all likelihood beating her own letter announcing her return.

"A surprise," she said, turning and smiling at him without breaking her stride. "Do please get some tea ready, I'll only be a moment in the gardens."

She didn't stop to see if he obeyed, though his footsteps no longer followed her. He may think his mistress a fool, but none of that mattered in the slightest compared to reaching the greenhouse. She didn't even know if Mr. Seoyaln was still here, but she tried to keep her head high. And despite her haste, she did feel a certain *freedom*, too. Even if she failed, even if he hated her forever, she had changed. Something inside her had finally blossomed, a seed pushing toward the light. And in that moment of possibility, there was … everything.

As she crossed the grounds, the greenhouse looked more immaculate than ever, though there seemed to be no trace of Mr. Seoyaln. His usual stool where he worked, his little notebook; it had all been seemingly scrubbed away. Had he really gone after all? For a moment she very nearly cried, as if she'd become a little girl again, stomping her foot at Father. But then she heard his voice, her heart leaping at the sound in a way she never thought it would.

When she finally found him he was kneeling over a flower bed, his arm working furiously with a trowel, his waistcoat still properly buttoned, though a small damp spot had appeared behind his neck, and the muscles of his back pulled against his shirt in a way she hadn't seemed to notice before. She thought he'd turn at the click of her shoes, but he was in a trance, digging a circle around a tiny white flower.

"Mr. Seoyaln," she said, her voice sounding strange in her ears.

He turned around, starting before he sprang to his feet, wiping his hands together.

"Lady Shuwayel," he stammered, bowing as he ran a hand through his hair. "I'm so very sorry. I wanted to be gone before you returned, it's only that the root rot is back in the erindelles, and I thought… Well, um …"

He paused, tilting his head to the side.

"Are you … quite all right?" he asked, raising a hand as if to take her by the arm before thinking better of it.

"I suppose I've never been better," she said, smiling. "Assuming, that is, you'll forgive me?"

He smiled, too, mirroring her, his eyes taking on a shine in the afternoon sun. How had she never noticed their marvelous chestnut color before?

"I'm afraid it's I who needs to be forgiven," he said, bowing again. "It was a kindness you did me, allowing me to stay on after your dear father passed. And, well, it was not my place to pass judgment on you. As any member of this staff knows, you're a marvelous woman, and I admit I can be a bit … dogmatic."

"I would use the world self-righteous," she said, grinning. "Though," she added quickly before his smile could disappear, "such things are only a problem if one fails to be right. And I don't think I've ever met a man more right than you, Mr. Seoyaln."

He raised an eyebrow at that, chuckling.

"I'm afraid I'll need you to elaborate," he said. "I was beginning to fear there wasn't an ounce of rightness in me, fleeing from these gardens like a coward."

Her heart seemed fit to leap from her chest, but she couldn't bear another moment of letting the truth hide right beneath her nose. For once, her plans and her schemes could rest on nothing but the truth, laid bare and stripped to nothing, the truth to save or damn her, judged with no regard for pomp nor circumstance. She forced herself to step forward and take his hand, the warmth and the dirt feeling like the first real thing she'd ever touched.

"You see," she said, her tongue suddenly feeling like wool. "I'm afraid I … love you, Mr. Seoyaln. I'm not sure I deserve you after the treatment you received in my service, but you saw the truth of who I was — who I ought to be — when no one else could. You are a man of honor and a man of goodness, and if you'll have me, I really must insist you never leave my side."

He laughed so heartily that, for a moment, she thought it would be the cruelest rejection of her life. But just as suddenly she was in his arms, spinning like a schoolgirl before he lowered her down, taking her face in his hands and kissing her, her body seeming to melt against him. It was everything Celanren's kiss was not, full of passion, yes, but tenderness too. A kiss that felt both safe and on fire at once, a kiss that could be trusted.

"I've loved you every day since I first set eyes on you," he said, finally pulling away. He kept his face close, as if afraid she'd disappear, his breath hot against her cheek. "I meant what I said in my letter. You are the best woman I've ever known, and if you'll have me, I'm yours forever."

She reached out and held his cheek, running her thumb over his face. Her face felt strained by her smile, the moment too big to hold within herself. Was this what love was meant to feel like? It was nothing like a ball, loud and chaotic, every eye on her. This was a deafening of the world, an eternal moment where only they existed.

"I think I'll need you to keep that promise," she said. "I suppose we won't lose Borimol, but I won't be a baroness much longer if we're to be wed."

"I daresay not," he said, laughing. "Though, I've always thought you'd make a good duchess, even if the duke in question wasn't always to my liking."

She frowned at him. Now was hardly the time to be making sport of her. Unless … what in Essomuai's name did he mean by her making a good duchess?

He seemed to notice the look on her face, cupping her check in his hand.

"Do you really not know?" he asked, pursing his lips. "I mean, I thought you were just making sport of me with all that 'Mr. Seoyaln' business — not that I minded, of course. At least it meant you noticed me, but …"

She suddenly noticed how low her jaw had dropped, and she snapped it closed. Still, she couldn't help but shake her head, a hand going to her temple.

"You're saying," she began, pointing at him, "that you are …"

"A duke," he said, nodding. "Or next year, anyway. I suppose you wouldn't have heard of our estates in Welenforn — they're farther north than Fire House lands, believe it or not. But my uncle, Lord Kilchuyeon, is set to retire on his eightieth birthday next year, and at that point I would, well … be a duke, I suppose."

"And I a duchess …" she added, staring off into space.

"I'm sorry," he said, chuckling. He took her by the shoulder, squeezing it. "It really is rather funny if you think about it, though. There's perhaps nothing more quintessentially your father than hiring an heir to work the gardens and never mentioning it to you."

"I think you're right," she said, a smile finally forcing its way through her shock. Remembering herself, she took his arm. "I hope you don't mistake me for disappointed. If anything, you've made yourself too eligible for me. I rather feel like a child who's stolen away with the pastry tray. I hardly expected my moral awakening to come with a duchy."

She shook her head, hitting him on the arm.

"I hope you're grateful," she said, "seeing as how I was prepared to throw over my position for you."

"Oh yes," he said with a grin, "I do believe I'll have a lot to be grateful for." He took her by the hand heading toward the exit. "Come on, I have my grandmother's bracelet somewhere in the cottage and you may want it before we tell the whole village."

They emerged onto the grass, the most familiar place in her life suddenly radically changed. She felt the eyes of the house on her, the staff no doubt noticing her arm in his, but she felt only pleasure at the thought — not to mention a surprising amount of pride. She would reign at Borimol with this man, the estates no longer bereft of the goodness she'd thought lost with Father's passing. But as they approached the tiny cottage she'd thought all too fitting for 'Mr. Seoyaln,' she suddenly felt the shock anew.

"I don't think I should find anything you do surprising any longer," she said. "But why did you take this post? You could have done a hundred other things while you waited for your title."

"I suppose," he said, "I needed to know if something else could be possible." He stopped, turning toward her. "We've done nothing to earn all this, won no battles to gather titles to our names. We're simply descended from men and women whose greatness always felt too distant from the little blood they left behind. And I thought one day, what if all of it just disappeared? Some raiders coming over the western seas and razing it all to the ground. What would that make it but a dream? And if it were a dream … what would you wish you'd done when you woke up?"

He smiled, shaking his head.

"I suppose you'd better stop me before I go on rambling again. I do believe you called me self-righteous not a moment ago?"

She pushed him on the shoulder, though she held his hand too tightly for the gesture to push him away entirely.

"Don't assume I won't find it endearing now," she said. "You may find yourself with a wife you can't get free of. Still, you sound just like Father — and maybe that's what drove me mad about you. But after seeing those poor souls in town …"

She shook her head, meeting his eyes.

"I promise for the rest of our days, we'll use this place to serve the people who need us. No matter the profit, my lands are yours, and your dreams are mine."

"And yours mine," he said, leaning in to kiss her again. She let herself melt away, the summer suddenly seeming unbearably hot despite the shade of the cottage.

THE END

Epilogue

Finally, the summer drifted past, and all its heat and ferocity washed away under the autumn rains rolling in from the coast. But on the day of Cullesil's wedding, there was only sunshine, the leaves of Borimol showing a dozen different colors as they waved in the cool breeze.

"Are you sure you know what you're doing?" Vorseyai called to Seoyaln where he drove the horses at the front of the phaeton.

"I seem to recall picking you up in the rain with no problem not so many months ago," he said, turning just long enough to give her a smug wink. Jeotolm was off helping Cullesil ferry her mob of guests to the wedding, and Seoyaln seemed particularly proud of driving in his stead.

"Hmph," she scoffed, folding her arms. "Call me foolish if you wish, but I dare say my strategy worked. I did manage to attract a gallant man in the rain, whether he knew it or not."

"You have me there," he said raising his hat.

"Just don't get too comfortable up there," she said. "Once I have our children I'm not letting you break your neck with these horses!"

He didn't turn around again, but something about his shoulders told her he was laughing.

Before long, they reached Cullesil's lands—and remarkably, in one piece—they reached Cullesil's lands and turned onto the long gravel drive, the house standing out against the sky. Already it seemed Lord Porsulair was making good on his promise, the entire drive lined with massive pumpkins of every size and shape, their leaves carefully painted gold for the wedding.

They parked with little fanfare, walking behind the house where there were two rows of chairs set up on the pavilion, all of it leading up to the wedding altar, the giant triangle of glass like a crystal tent glinting in the sun. The usher showed them to their seats — in the front row, of course — as they waited for the couple to arrive from their private signing. It couldn't be a long wait, though; the afternoon sun was very nearly at the point where it'd sit right atop the prism, bathing the couple in Essomuai's light.

Finally, the back door of the house opened and Lord Porsulair emerged, waving to the crowd as he walked toward the altar. He looked to be about the happiest man in the entire world — second only to Seoyaln himself, of course, whose hand gripped hers tightly next to the folds of her dress. The priest followed next, his formal robes looking tight against his girth. But not even Child Malpiyeon's presence could detract from Cullesil's radiance as she came into the light.

She looked … stunning. Vorseyai had seen the dress at the tailor's, of course, but it was quite another thing entirely to see Cullesil standing beneath the glass. Dark green was such a tricky color — not that Grass House green would do her own complexion any favors — but under the dappled light, it looked like the most sumptuous thing you could imagine. She wore a scrollwork tiara on her head, and circled around her hands was the wedding wreath, the just-picked hay woven to perfection.

A man in mauve livery came out last, standing just beside the prism with his hands folded behind his back. That would be the Shadow House scribe, then … To think Cullesil almost turned down the love of her life because she didn't think herself worthy of being a bloody countess! She nodded her chin in the scribe's direction, Seoyaln finally pulling his eyes away from the happy couple.

"I suppose we'll need one of those from Sky House, eh?" she whispered.

"Perhaps," he said, grinning, "though I could live with being a Grass House baron, too."

She squeezed his hand, looking back to the front as the sun finally tilted into position. Suddenly, the prism glowed like a lighthouse, a wide swath of golden light showering the couple as it spilled onto the grass. The tears of joy on Cullesil's face seemed to sparkle, her smile widening as she held onto Lord Porsulair, looking as if she'd float away without his hands to hold her down.

For once, everything felt right. There was nothing to scheme about, no chiding from Mother's voice in her head. There was only Yuljeom and Borimol, the huge golden fields stretching until they met the eternity of the ocean. And in that blissful moment, the goddess felt like more than an idea, her light washing over them along with … *hope*. No matter how foolish or harried their lives, no matter how lost they became, there would always be another door to open. And like light, waiting to banish the darkness, there would always be love.

THE BORIMOL PLAINS

Dear reader,

Thank you so much for reading my story! It means the world to me. It may not seem like much, but I truly believe the empathy and kindness it takes to dive into a story can change the world.

If you wouldn't mind taking the time to leave me an honest review, that would be incredibly helpful. As an indie author, knowing what you loved (or hated!) will help others find (or avoid!) this book.

If you'd like to follow me on instagram, I'm at @jhtomen and love to hear from readers there, too. I admittedly don't post that often (working on new books for you!) but I will occasionally post cute pics of cats or talk about book launches. Thank you for everything you are and everything you do. May joy and light always find you.

JH Tomen

For AR

Love always blossoms where you least expect it.
And in its wake we are renewed.

et tui amóris in eis ignem accénde
renovábis fáciem terræ

www.ingramcontent.com/pod-product-compliance
Lightning Source LLC
Chambersburg PA
CBHW060336310726
48976CB00007B/2578